About the Author

Christina Deodat was born in Guyana, and immigrated to Ontario, Canada as a shy high school student. She quickly found her inspiration and love of Victorian literature in g

rade twelve English after reading Austen's Pride and Prejudice. This novel inspired her to pursue a university degree in English and Education. She always viewed writing as a secret passion and longed for an inspiration to start her career as an author. This came after the birth of her son, where she took the elusive Estella and provided her with a story of her own. As the saying goes… the rest is history.

Greater Expectation:

The Intimate Confession
of an
Heiress

Christina Deodat

Greater Expectation:

The Intimate Confession
of an
Heiress

Vanguard Press

VANGUARD PAPERBACK

© Copyright 2023
Christina Deodat

The right of Christina Deodat to be identified as author of
this work has been asserted by her in accordance with the
Copyright, Designs and Patents Act 1988.

All Rights Reserved

No reproduction, copy or transmission of this publication
may be made without written permission.
No paragraph of this publication may be reproduced,
copied or transmitted save with the written permission of the
publisher, or in accordance with the provisions
of the Copyright Act 1956 (as amended).

Any person who commits any unauthorised act in relation to
this publication may be liable to criminal
prosecution and civil claims for damages.

A CIP catalogue record for this title is
available from the British Library.

ISBN 978 1 83794 026 4

*This is a work of fiction. Names, characters, businesses, places, events and
incidents are either the product of the author's imagination or used in a
fictitious manner. Any resemblance to actual persons, living or dead, or actual
events is purely coincidental.*

*Vanguard Press is an imprint of
Pegasus Elliot Mackenzie Publishers Ltd.*
www.pegasuspublishers.com

First Published in 2023

**Vanguard Press
Sheraton House Castle Park
Cambridge England**

Printed & Bound in Great Britain

Introduction

This is my first literary work and I am very excited to share it publicly. I would like to first acknowledge my love for Victorian literature and romantic fiction. Authors like Austen, Hardy, the Bronte sisters and Thackeray have inspired me to dream and create. Whether that is writing a novel or being a hopeless romantic, I thank these writers for creating worlds where goodness prevails and soulmates are destined to be together. As a modern woman I know we just cannot sit around and wait for Mr. Darcy to come knocking at our door. So, this book will forever be dedicated to all the hopeless romantics who are strong, independent and refuse to settle for mediocre. That perfect partner who will inspire, motivate and love you for who you are is out there. I also owe a debt of gratitude to authors like E. L. James who did not shy away from sex or BDSM but embraced it in their works and created popular fiction that is enjoyed by many.

I would like to thank from the bottom of my heart the few people who knew about this endeavour and helped me along the way without any judgement. To my supportive parents, Deodat and Shirley, who always encouraged me to use my university degree and follow my dreams of becoming a writer. Mom and dad, I strive to make you proud, every day. To my unofficial proof reader, Peter Koroloff, thank you for your steadfast support throughout this journey. Thank you for reading some of my chapters and making sound corrections. Also, I want to thank my lovely children, Spencer and Amelia, who inspire me every day to persevere and always reach for the stars. I will forever be too embarrassed to share this book with the two of you. Lastly, thank you Mr. Charles Dickens for creating an inspirational masterpiece that transcends time. This has been quite the journey and I hope I brought justice to the mysteriously fascinating character, Estella Havisham.

Chapter 1

And born I did: a screaming, scrawny child of six pounds and zero ounces, given up at birth by my crack head mother who decided to overdose and die during my delivery; and of course, no trace of a father. That was my beginning, and this is my story.

***

"Fuck him, we will liquidize his company. Trust me, he won't know what will hit him. The fucker wants to underestimate me then let him." I'm on the phone with my second in command. He's fierce and looks exactly like the CEO of one of the biggest telecommunication companies in North America. It's a privately traded company with a board, where I own 99 % of the stocks. That's right baby, I'm the CEO, not him. I founded and I am solely running this company. But, I like having a board as they keep me grounded.

I graduated top of my class five years ago from the Wharton School of Business of the University of Pennsylvania. With many right investments, and here I am—Chief Executive Officer at age twenty-eighty. OK, so my benefactor invested the first three million, but our net worth last year was over 150 million dollars. We are doing well. I am proud of my work.

That's about all that I'm proud of though. I have a very peculiar outlook on life thanks to my dear benefactor. I'm not complaining, and to be honest I won't have it any other way. But I am bored ever since my last male interest. He was two years younger, and it didn't last long. I wanted his full submission with no attachments. He wanted a sugar mama, which he got in some respects for services rendered. He also wanted an attachment, which he did not get, and his nagging personality made me cut him loose. To be fair he did not fully understand the relationship, although he claimed he did.

OK, me in a nutshell—I'm a cold person. I do not want or even understand the idea of love. It does not exist to me. My beliefs are that there are no couples out there that are truly in love with each other. It's just a game to make people feel less alone and more secure. I do not need that game. I prefer getting a partner for my sexual needs, then cut him loose when I'm done. I don't need attachments nor feelings; I just want physical. That's the way I like it. I'm no whore either; I am very picky with whom I sleep with, and I usually will keep them under contract for at least a year. I do a full background check and of course a confidentiality agreement. I do not do relationships, hearts or flowers. My life this way is rewarding and its freedom. But as I sit in my huge office, I realize that I'm bored. My usual partners are around my age, and on the surface, they are aggressive and assertive men, some would even say dominants. I enjoy the challenge of breaking them into subs. Although, I wouldn't classify myself as a BDSM person per say, I do enjoy aspects of it. I love and crave control. It's who I am and will always be. I'm also a bit of a sadist because I cannot empathize with people. One usually needs to have feelings and emotions to do so, and I do not.

This attitude stems from Adela Havisham, the woman who adopted me at birth. She has a lot of hate in her and made sure it rubbed off onto me when I was a child. This training started when I was around eleven; Adela introduced me to a young boy named Philip. She even toyed with the idea of being his benefactor. Like me, he was an orphan who was being raised by his older sister. One of our gardeners brought him to our home and he fell immediately in love with me. In return I was cold and sterile towards him; I never reciprocated any sort of feelings towards him, but just tolerated his presence enough to keep him coming back just like Adela wanted.

I was desensitized by sex and all the things teenagers might be interested from age twelve. Before that age Adela, my benefactor, raised me in a cold, non-loving environment, where we met once a day for dinner. The rest of the time I was privately educated by tutors, professors and professionals who came to the house. As a baby I even had a wet nurse, and Adela saw me twice a week during that stage of my life.

I did not fully understand the power I had over the opposite sex. My training all started when I turned twelve and I went on my first trip to the Adela's chateau in the South of France. I was excited. It was exactly as breath taking as I imagined. Nestled in the French countryside, this grand estate was meant for royalties. It sat on over fifty acres of pristine real estate with roaring hills, and beautiful lakes. In the summer the estate came to life with fragrant smells and its lush forest. I loved going for walks on the property, and swimming in the lake, pretending to be a siren who would drown the sailors as they pass by. Yes, I know—morbid for a twelve-year-old.

My training began after my first month there, when Adela started my lesson on human nature by sending me to a brothel in Nice. I saw everything and anything you can imagine. She paid good money every summer so I'm aware what young people want with the same or opposite sex. The carnal undertakings at these places vary from your missionary and boring sex to BDSM, to orgies, to gay sex etc. I was initially scared and freaked out, but after multiple times of seeing these types of relations I got curious then bored. Ms. Havisham enjoyed all my reactions to the sceneries, but never allowed me to be touched by these people. According to her she was raising a seemingly lady, who will ruin the lives of all men who stupidly fall in love with me. Adela has an interesting history that I will divulge later. The point of these brothels was to remove feelings and emotions from sex; instead, she wanted me to see sex for what it truly is—simply a physical act of pleasure.

After my first summer in France, Adela kept encouraging Philip to pursue me and made him believe that she would financially support him. He became her guinea pig towards my training. She loved every moment of our interactions, and she thrived on his vulnerability and the pain I brought him. This went on for a few years. I tolerated his presence at our house every Sunday and in some sort of way, I looked forward to his visits. This went on until I became engaged to a man named Tom. After Tom proposed to me, I quickly sent Philip a nude pic from the neck down. I did not see him for a week after, and when I did, I told him of my engagement. This was the ultimate betrayal. I told Adela what I did, and she was proud of me. Looking back now I am ashamed of how I treated him because he was a kind soul who didn't deserve to be taunted by Adela and myself.

***

I pause as I feel tired from this call. I'm too tired to be bothered by Winston and Wail Inc—the company I'm dealing with. I want to go for a walk. I am disgusted that men treat me this way because I'm a woman! I earned all I have—woman or no woman. Cassandra, my assistant, wants to schedule an in-person meeting. I just want to crush him and tear apart his company. This company has a lucrative micro-chip factory in Costa Rica. They rival Microsoft, and considerably cheaper to deal with. Although, the board of directors are all middle-aged men who think it's ridiculous that I own my own globally traded telecommunication company and have second thoughts giving up control to a woman. The deal is almost done, as I've made an offer they cannot refuse. I should let George Darcy, my VP, take care of this, but I'm very hands on when it comes to big deals. I abruptly end the call with this man because I know the company is mine! I take a deep breath, but I realize I need to clear my head.

I decide to leave my office and go for a walk, only to find a crisp and cold early afternoon, but I don't feel it. I love the cold; I can breathe in the cold when I feel tense and bored with life.

It's been three years since my divorce. I should feel bad for my ex, but I warned him the day he married me. I told him I am a heartless bitch that will crush him. I told him that on our wedding night and reminded him during our divorce proceedings. If I had a heart, I would have felt some sort of empathy for him. I blame my benefactor of course. Suddenly, I am startled from my reverie by a commotion of some sort, which I have no interest in. I need something or someone to distract me.

As I head back, I remember my one-thirty p.m. meeting. Cassandra is waiting for me with a stack full of files. She whispers, "He's here. He was early. I showed him into the board office." I frowned because I hate being hurried, and she notices. She asks, "Would you like him in your office instead?"

I say, "Sure." Then I go into my office and what a view: prime real-estate in Manhattan. I pull the Templeton file from the stack she gave me. It's a small publishing company that I recently acquired partly due to the previous pandemic. I want to keep the company for a bit then sell it to the highest bidder. It's a flip; I have done it a few times and was rewarded for my patience. The company is doing OK, but not great as they didn't properly transition over to e-books and online publishing. If I give it a face lift, get some talented editors, give it an online presence, and tighten up what they produce, I might be able to make a good profit. I don't know the lawyer they are using for the sale, and with my line of work I know most of the corporate asshole lawyers.

Cassandra shows him into my office. Without raising my head from the file, I mutter, "Sorry to keep you waiting. I went through the agreement and my lawyers have a copy of the sale. So how can I help you, Mr?" As I raise my head, I notice he is attractive, and a full head of hair for a change. I'm guessing he's thirty, around my age, too young to be the sole counsel on this file. He looks nervous, like I'm going to bite. I would, but I never mix business with pleasure.

He starts off with, "Donaldson. Ms. Havisham, thank you for meeting me. I am here because my client would like a personal favour. Templeton Publishing has been in his family for over fifty years. He would like to keep his daughter as Chief Editor. She is highly qualified and knows all their clients well. She has single handily helped with the publication of some top sellers." Are you kidding me? Fuck no! She is on my hit list to fire first. She is only

Chief Editor because daddy owns the company. This request is preposterous. He must know this. He does because I can see the nervousness in his posture. He knows she is a no talent hack, only there because of daddy.

I commence with, "Mr. Donaldson, I understand your client's request, but cannot make any promises or personal favours at this time. I am looking forward to acquiring this publishing company, but I will need to assess the talents and the 'what not's' at Templeton myself." I see the disappointment in his eyes. He would have been a hero to Mr. Templeton if I granted this favour. But any shrewd businessperson would say no. I continue, "So please apologize to Mr. Templeton and inform him that I will not be granting this request. As the new proprietor, I will do as I see fit with my company. Is there anything else, Mr. Donaldson?"

He looks down at his files, defeated, but of course not surprise by my response. He fumbles with his papers. He looks anxious now. I don't think he wants to end this meeting. Cassandra will pop in shortly …to announce my next appointment. What is he thinking? I bet he's good in bed, maybe he even has a big package… mmmm, intriguing! His eyes are green and he has thick dark brown hair. He's tall too, maybe 6'2". I would love to climb on top of him, but he speaks again: "no Ms. Havisham. That's all I wanted to discuss at this time. Thank you for seeing me. I will let my client know." There is chemistry. I can feel a little tingle when I look into his eyes. He's disappointed this meeting is ending, and I'll admit, so am I.

Cassandra opens the door and interrupts our talk by saying, "Ms. Havisham your 2:30 appointment is waiting." I respond in a nonchalant way, "thank you. We are not done yet. I'll let you know when we are." She is stunned. I end with, "that will be all." She closes the door behind her. Back to Mr. Donaldson—"please call me Estella. So why did old man Templeton really sell his company, anyways?" of course I know the answer, but I want to see what he's going to say. He looks perplexed for a second, then says, "to be frank I can't really divulge that info. Solicitor/client privilege. Sorry." This is good—he's trustworthy. He's meek, timid even, but has what some would call honour and loyalty.

I continue, "ah of course, I'm sorry for asking. Are you a new hire to Mr. Templeton's team? Sorry for prying. But I knew the firm he used before." Of course, I know he's selling this company because he's heavily indebted and can't afford a big law firm handling this sale. Mr. Donaldson responds, "he wanted something more intimate and smaller. This company meant a lot to him. I think he wanted to go out dignified." Translation, he couldn't afford the big law firm bill because his silly daughter ran him a mock. I quickly say, "OK sure. Sounds great. Nice meeting you. I'll be at the closing." Enough of this, I have a meeting with a Japanese investor who wants to dump five million into my safe drinking water project waiting in the lobby.

As he puts together the paperwork to leave, he says, "I'm sure your attorneys have advised you that you don't have to be there. It's quite boring. However, I would love to see you again. So, I think you should come." Is this his attempt at flirting because it's sad. I sweetly tell him, "thanks for the invite, I like the hands-on approach, so I'll be there." I was not planning on going, but what the fuck! I want to see him squirm and he's cute. "Ok great. I'll see you soon. It was really a pleasure meeting you," he comments with his broad shoulders, and muscular physique, but not bulging either. He is very good looking. I quickly say, "you too. Goodbye, Mr. Donaldson." He lingers then says, "bye, Ms. Estella."

Cassandra is stalking outside my office and as soon as he's out, she slithers in. She quietly says in a curious tone, "what was that?! Mr. Yamamtoo has been waiting for twenty minutes. You are always on time." True, I'm very punctual. But he's cute and I'm bored. I ignore her and open the door greeting Mr. Yamamtoo with my girlish smile and award winning "Kon'nichiwa." He smiles. He's a nice older gentleman, who's is probably having a sexual fantasy about me in his head. I know I look hot, with a red inspired Japanese style dress. This will be easy.

Chapter 2

I got divorced about three years ago. I met him when I was sixteen years old. He was handsome and athletic with the all-American charm. I don't care for his type, but Ms. Havisham insisted that I married him. I tolerated him at best when I first met him. He was too cocky and arrogant for his own good. But he had wealth and most importantly he had a good name. He was the complete opposite of Philip, who like me was an orphan with poor parentage and no wealth. The Havishams are old money from the old world—a highly respectable name that I bear. Havisham International is a multibillion-dollar real estate development corporation that was founded by Adela's father, who migrated here as a child from England. His father had major landownership in England and was also some sort of a lavish land developer. This company and all its earnings were passed down to Adela upon her father's death. Since she has no children, she has named me as her sole heiress—an inheritance that is beyond my understanding.

I don't care for frivolous things like a name, but Ms. Havisham insisted I marry someone with equal status or better if I ever got married to begin with. Although the Havishams were hard to match in name and wealth, Tom

Calloway was close. His family have a very respectable name and they have a lot of money. Although his family was not pleased with me because my adoptive status, Tom fell hard for me as he was quite in love with the image I projected onto him at the time.

We were both from New Hampshire, and because of the wealth and status of both families, we always tend to see each other at social events and balls. At first, he was captivated by my looks. He always came to our home, and he wanted to escort me to charity events and places. Havisham knew at once he was to be my husband. I didn't think he would go against his family's dictum and marry me, so, I kept him at arm's length. I was even cold at times to him, but he was persistent and finally I allowed him to take me on a typical boring dinner date. He conversed as best as he could. He listened to me regal about my summers at the Havisham's chateau in the south of France (not the whore houses part). He was even pleased I spoke French and played the piano. I knew he was measuring me up as a submissive wife, and I, on the other hand, was utterly bored by him, but carried on like I cared.

It was evident on our first date the sex he was expecting would not happen until I had a secure relationship with him, and yes that meant marriage.

My reaction to Tom stems from my distaste for men and women because of my benefactor; she taught me how to hate. I am her perfect weapon against humanity. She grew me up to be accomplished, beautiful and to be desired by everyone—men, women and children. She also taught me to hate everyone. From the minute she adopted me I was fully submerged into her disdain for humanity. She wanted me to crush and ruin as many lives as possible. And I must say, so far I've made her proud. Apart from Philip, I had many suitors who came to our home before I married Tom, but I had no interest whatsoever. Adela enjoyed seeing me crush these young men's hopes in her presence.

Tom was different because of his pedigree. He was the type of boy she wanted me to nurture until he was an adult then strip him of his manhood. She loved seeing this heir to a powerful family fall in love with me. After graduating high school (which was a private all boys school), Tom went to Harvard. He studied Politics and Law. During this time our courtship was unconventional to say the least. It was sterile and cold. We did not go on many dates, but in his own way, he did the romantic junk to me. Tom assumed I was like the girls he dated, and I would simply fall in line with whatever he wanted. I feigned interest and continued doing so up until our wedding night, at which point everything changed. I also suspected Tom fooled around with girls at his school, but I didn't care. I didn't have to fuck him, so it was a win for me. I always knew Tom was an arrogant son of a bitch.

After he passed the Bar, we got married (to the dismay of his parents). He is an only child and was prepped for greatness. He is their hope and joy. Looking back, I do feel some remorse for him.

I remember his look on our wedding night—shock. He had no idea the meek little thing that just married him was his worst nightmare. I confronted him in our suite about the women, and I promised to cut off his balls if I ever caught him cheating again. I really didn't care about the women, but I would not be embarrassed by his cheating. He also wanted me to be a stay-at-home wife. He expected me to quit Wharton and dedicate my life to his goals. That was a laughable idea, which I informed him during our honeymoon.

I remember the first time we had sex—which was on our wedding night. When we got into our suite, I took him to the bed then cuffed him, tied up his feet, and gagged him. Shock cannot express what I saw on his face, but he was curious to see where this was going so, he let me do it. I bought handcuffs for this occasion because I knew he was strong. I got a ridding crop and wailed it all over his chest. When I ungagged him, he was livid with anger, and yes fear. I started my mission to make this strong man into my submissive. He yelled at me to uncuff him and threatened to hit me, but his threats didn't faze me.

I got ice from the mini fridge in our room and rubbed it all over his body; soothing where the blows hit him. He asked me to release him so he can show me what a real man can do, but I told him I wanted control and to be quiet. Then I gently kissed him everywhere. I finally took off my wedding dress to reveal my white lace trim silk lingerie. He had never seen me like this before and his eyes bulged at this sight. He wasn't mad any more but intrigued. I kissed him hard and when I pulled away, he longed for more. I removed his shirt and exposed my muscular husband, then I worked on his pants. I wanted to take in his nakedness. He looked like a man chiselled out of the finest material. He looked good. Maybe I can grow to love him, but I quickly dismissed that idea.

I slowly took off his pants, fully noticing his penis growing in length. Then I took up the ridding crop and mashed it hard against his manhood. He screamed in pain and a bevy of cursing ensued. I kissed his penis gently sucking the tip. He calmed down and relaxed again. I started kissing up his belly and chest stopping at his nipples. I locked my lips on his right nipple and sucked hard. Then I clamped my teeth around it. He bled and started screaming once again. So, I slowly took off my bra and then fondled my right breast. Then trail my index finger down my belly into my panties. I gently massaged myself, taking full satisfaction that Tom was silent, entranced and completely seduced. I spoke: "You are mine now, Tom. I own you. You will do what I say from henceforth. Acknowledge."

All he said was, "Yes." Then I climb on top of him, putting his very enlarged penis into my mouth. He moaned and I gave him a stinging slap on his penis.

"Don't make a sound." I continued to suck his penis but stopped just when I knew he was going to come. "Not yet," I whispered. He did not protest. I took my panties off and slid myself on top of his face so he can lick me. Then I slid back down his chest, pausing to rub my clit onto his rock-hard abs. I then got off him and held his penis into my hands and sucked it long and hard for another couple of minutes. I lowered myself unto his hard penis. He was too big and I was too tight. The only thought going through my head was you are a virgin you idiot. He will know, and your sexual prowess will all be for nothing. I needed to conquer him. I got off because I knew he felt how tight I was. I did not want him to know I was a virgin. So, I sat on him again; it felt so fucking tight and painfully. But I did the motions: slowly up and down, then faster. I grit my teeth and I knew he was going to come... he screamed my name when he reached his climax.

I hated every second of it. When he was fully inside me, I felt disgusted by him, and despised him even more. Tom became mankind and I wanted nothing to do with him or any other man. I finally had sex with my husband. It was underwhelming, plus I did not orgasm. As he laid there I got up and undid his cuffs. He had bruises on both his wrists, there was a bit of blood on his arm and the sheets possibly from both of us. He rubbed his hands then looked at me. I stood there naked and proud. I felt strong because if he was going to hit me, I would hit him back. I will never be the meek wife he thought he married and as we looked at each, I knew he realized who I really was. He hugged me, but I could not return it. I said, "When we go to our new house you will be sleeping in the guest room across from the library." This house was a gift from Adela and many of our staff were hand chosen by Adela (one would say they were her spies). He was not stunned, as he whispered, "OK, we will talk tomorrow." I think he was just tired because he closed his eyes and was asleep.

This began my five years of marriage to the mighty and powerful Tom Calloway. He and I had a lengthy conversation the next day. We met in his office, and I treated this as what it really was —a contract. He understood I was not what he expected; not the hearts and flower little woman he thought he fell in love with. Instead, I told him that I will draw up a contact as to what I expected out of this marriage. I wanted total control in the bedroom and all aspects outside of the bedroom. However, I understood his reputation so I would allow him to continue on with his tirade of masculinity in public. But in private I will call all the shots. If he disagreed, I would simply leave him.

I think he agreed to my request because he found a new sort of love or admiration for me. Plus, I think he was curious as to where this would go, and he would be quite embarrassed if I did leave him after a few days of marriage. In any case, he readily accepted my contract and was willing to sign a confidentiality agreement (although he thought the confidentiality agreement was a bit much). I also outlined no extra marital affair without my permission. I told him I knew about these women. He was surprised I knew about his escapades while he was at Harvard, but he agreed to my request, citing men had needs and I did not have sex with him before. I couldn't care less about who he fucked, but if I'm fucking him, I should be the only one; I don't share. This monogamy had nothing to do with love or feelings.

For the first few years we got a good feel for each. Tom kept his promises; no extra marital affairs (I hired a private investigator to ensure this was true), and more importantly he gave me complete control, which I rewarded him immeasurably in the bedroom.

My sexual knowledge from the French Riviera just poured freely into my marriage with Tom. He allowed me to beat him, tie him up, gag him and blind fold him. Sex became fun and pleasurable with Tom. I remember distinctly going to a Midsummer Night's mascaraed charity ball at the Governor's House in New Hampshire. We went upstairs to a bedroom, where I proceeded to unzip Tom's pants and commanded him to take them off. He simply said, "Yes." I wanted him to keep his shirt on so I can focus on his penis. He started growing in front of me and it made me feel warm and tingly inside. I kneeled in front of him and grabbed his manhood in my right hand. It felt good and hard.

I barked, "Don't move, put your hands behind your back." I ran my tongue down his shafts, flicking the end of his penis against my lips. I saw him take a deep breath. "Don't move," I warned. I got up to take off his shirt and pushed him onto the bed. I began sucking his penis again, back and forth. I took off my panties and hiked up my dress then sat pressing his penis down. I was very wet and I wanted to rub his penis on my clit. He moaned some more. I gently kissed his belly button and worked my way up his chest, then his mouth. I always kissed him hard and ravenous. I told him I wanted him on top and he proceeded to eat my vagina, while I rocked back and forth. He slid his tongue deep inside me, and then out, then in, flicking it against my clit. I felt the tension build inside me. I knew I was about to come, so I held on to Tom's shoulders finding my release.

I collapsed on to him for a few seconds. Then I came off the bed and took off my dress. I stood in front of this man naked. I started kissing his penis again. He grew bigger in size. I then climbed on top of him again, this time putting the tip of his penis inside me. He moaned and moved his hands, I restrained his hands and placed it above his head. I then asked, "How badly do you want to be inside me" and he responded.

"More than anything; I want all of you." I'm indifferent to Tom's sex talk, so I told him to shut up and lowered myself completely onto him. He moaned and started pushing up on to me. I braced both of my hands against his shoulders and proceeded to go up and down on him. Slowly I started riding him, then faster. When he was about to come, I stopped and got off him. He yelped "No." But I ignored his desire. I put his penis into my mouth and started sucking hard for twenty seconds then went back on top of him. I wanted him to see all of my beauty and glory. His eyes looked hungry, and I went faster and faster. He was about to explode, and I felt that tension build up inside me too. He came gloriously with quite the moaning, followed shortly after by me. We collected ourselves and went back down to the party without anyone knowing. We did this frequently at public outings and at friends' homes—it was exciting for both of us.

At this point in our marriage Tom had given up all the power to me. He genuinely enjoyed having sex and being dominated in and out of the bedroom. The sex was good. So good that my PI reported monthly that he was not having any extra marital affairs. I essentially broke this dominant man into being my submissive.

Apart from the bedroom, our marriage was running smoothly so to speak. He agreed to my conditions. I mean he kept his macho image in the public eye, but I called all the shots. At the beginning it was hard giving up control to me, but he saw the merits. His career flourished, despite working for his father's law firm. His public persona began to soar. Our end goal was for him to get into politics, but to do that I wanted him to be established as a great corporate lawyer. Plus, he was twenty-eight at the time.

With both of our social connections and networking capabilities, we were invited to the most exclusive parties, charity events and social gatherings. It was a bit tiresome but that was what I wanted at the time—to establish ourselves as a strong power couple. We went to governors' balls, Geneva for charity events and even a presidential inauguration. His family warmed up to me, and I pretended to like them. They saw that I was taking their beloved son somewhere—high society and politics were exactly what they had in mind for dear Tom. As for Adela, I met up with her once a week to discuss my marriage. She was obviously thrilled Tom was in love with me and did what I wanted. If it wasn't for her, I would have left Tom sooner. I wouldn't have married him in the first place. This was all part of her plans.

Tom thanked his success in life to me. He had direction because of me. As for my career, I graduate from Wharton and made a bold purchase of a small telecommunication company that was on the brink of bankruptcy before my 25th birthday. It cost five million to clear one hundred percent of this company. I quickly wiped out the name and created my own image. I put the company out of commission for one year. I needed to research the telecommunication market and create my own image. Tom thought I didn't need to work, that I ought to be a stay-at-home wife and possibly think about starting a family with him. My response to this was—yuck. I couldn't imagine having children with Tom or anyone at this time in my life. The idea of bringing a child into this world made me want to vomit.

I declared to Tom very quietly, but stern, "Tom, I will be taking on this venture and will be the CEO of this telecommunication company. I will also be taking two million dollars from our account. Ms. Havisham will be giving me the rest to purchase the company."

Tom said, "That's a lot of money, Estella. Are you sure about this market? We could end up losing. And don't you have your hands full with Adele's company?" I simply told him.

"I don't own Adele company—it is not my creation. This will be a great venture and I've done my research. I will not sit at home waiting for you. I can also make a name for myself and would like to do this. Plus, I am not asking for permission, I'm informing you of my decision." Tom knew better than to proceed with this conversation; he knew the money was also mine and he knew I was too independent to depend on Adele or him.

He just said, "OK, Estella. If that's what you want to do, I support you."

"Thanks, Tom. I want this. Are we going to the Louvre for the Refugee Charity Ball? I would like to attend, but I know your schedule is tight." This was my way of changing the subject.

He responded, "It's on the weekend, so we can go. We can fly out on my dad's jet on Friday. I'll have Connie send you the info." Connie was his secretary, and I hated using anything belonging to his parents, but such a last-minute thing will be too much of a hassle to hire a private jet or get the Havisham's jet. So, his parents' will have to do.

The important part of that conversation was he agreed to let me use two million of our money to purchase my company… my baby. My head spun with all the possibilities for this company. I was researching the telecommunication market, contacting other companies and coming up with ideas. I investigated hiring people with the right background and knowledge to make this company a global powerhouse. Also, I needed to ask Adele for three million—I am her sole heiress, so I knew this was not an issue. Although I used both of their money, I wanted to start and create my own legacy and wealth. I did not want to be known as the wife of Tom Calloway or Adela's heiress. I wanted to be a strong, smart and independent businesswoman.

As for our philanthropy, we donated quite a bit. My personal causes are inhuman treatment to children. That have always been a keen interest to me partly because of being abandon at birth and being an orphan. Tom understood a selfish-aspect of charity—it was to further his career and probably make him feel like a decent human, but he, like his father, was quite slimy.

The Calloway men are lawyers, specifically corporate lawyers. They represent high profile companies in the US. Most of their clients are detestable even to me. I avoid socializing with these people and only do so when I must.

In a nutshell shell, that was my marriage to Tom. No passion, no love, just a good understanding and a good sex. And after a while I became bored of that arrangement. This was never going to be a permanent contract; Adela wanted Tom's complete devotion to me and then I needed to divorce him. I had no issues with this plan as I did not love Tom at all.

During the middle of our fifth year of marriage, I became restless. My company was picking up steam. Tom was also doing well, but our marriage was stagnant. We hardly saw each other, and at times our assistants made appointments for us to have dinner. I was always in New York, and Tom retained a mistress or two. I remember specifically flying in to confront him on this issue and to terminate our marriage.

We met at our house for dinner, I didn't mention the issue on the phone. I simply started the dinner by saying, "As you probably have guessed, I am here to talk about your mistress. That's great you found someone, but we are married." Tom's look was sad, and I did feel some sort of sorrow for him. Sorrow because he unfortunately fell in love with me. He could have made another woman happy, but I knew that was not possible any more.

He became a dominant with his affairs. My PI once reported that all the women he slept with looked like me and he would treat them terribly. Sigmund Freud would have had a field day with us. Tom said in a sternly yet gently voice, "I'm sorry I didn't keep my promise. But I know I am not hurting you, Estella. Nothing I do hurts you. You never loved me. I know you never really showed me love, but I really hoped that one day you would realize you were my world. I was in love with you (I still am), and would do anything to make you happy."

I began to say, "Tom I warned." But he continued, "Don't say anything Estella, not now. You will get your chance. Our relationship started as a fling. My family, as I'm sure you are fully aware, did not approve of our relationship. We were not supposed to be anything serious. But you captivated me with your strength and independence. Before I met you, I was a spoiled man with no care in the world. I enjoyed fucking women, drinking and partying. I did well at Harvard and I'm sure that was partly due to my parents' generous donations. My life was great. I needed a suitable wife and when I first saw you, like any man with a pulse I was blown away. I needed to have you. But you just wouldn't give it up. Fuck, if you screwed me, I would have been over you. But we had this weird relationship where you were so proper in front of everyone and didn't give a shit about the girly relationship when we were alone. Then that first night you fucked me... mind fucking blowing and yes, I knew you were a virgin. I also knew I was in love with you. I never saw myself as a man who follows his old lady's command, but for you Estella, I would do anything. I would only let you treat me like that—the hitting and tying up. I would only be your submissive.

"Everything was fine. I even researched my new BDSM sex life! I embraced it because of you. Although, I always thought you were cold, I really believed that you would eventually warm up to me. Years past and no real change, and shockingly I had no interest in anyone else. I lived and breadth whatever you wanted me to with the hope that one day you would see how devoted I was to you.

"I think what really broke me was that fucking company of yours. I made the biggest mistake by giving you that money to purchase that fucking company. It took whatever I had of you away from me."

I began to say, "Tom it wasn't... " But he cut me off again and continued in an eerily calm voice.

"Let me finish, Estella. I was so in love with you, and you didn't care or reciprocated any of it. I didn't know what to do; as you started traveling to New York, I began drinking." I knew this. He continued, "I mean lots, I had no one to talk to, so I turned to my father. He helped me put down the bottle. You stopped having sex with me. That crushed me again, so I focused my attention on the other women around me. They are a good outlet for me. I treat them how you treated me. I'm sure any psychiatrist would tell me how fucked up that was. But I don't care, Estella. All I want is you," he stopped talking.

I guess now it was my turn. I didn't want to deal with the end of my marriage like this. A quick email or message could have sufficed, but here I was listening to this man's confessional.

I took a deep breath then began, "Tom, I appreciate the honesty. But you cheated and broke your promise so there is no going back. I want a divorce. You knew I couldn't love you from day one. I never hid my feelings from you. I'm not going to sit here and explain my company either. I love what I have done with the company and will continue growing it. End of story, Tom. And as for our marriage, I'll have Peter Donovan draft up my terms. I don't want a big public messy divorce. I don't need that attention right now."

Tom commented quietly, "I don't want a divorce."

I continued, "There needn't be any fuss over this. We grew apart. I'm sure Peter can make a good, shared press statement from both of us. I would like this to be amicable." I snuck in 'us' because a press statement from both of us would be good to dodge prying eyes and rumours. We became page six regulars and the media always focused on our marriage and success.

It seemed like a century, but Tom finally said, "I won't cause you any stress if this is absolutely what you want. You can have everything as well. I know you earn a very good living and have quite a bit from your side. But you can take whatever you want; the houses, cottage, cars, boat, whatever you want. And you know my net worth. You can have it all, Estella." As I heard him speak, I felt disgusted by the thought of taking his money and properties, leaving him as a pauper. I didn't care about him, but I was too independent and proud to take anything from him.

"Tom, I want what is mine. I put a lot of thought and time into designing this house, so I want it. You can keep your cars, boat, apartment in Manhattan, cottage in Colorado and the house in Florida, and of course your net worth," I concluded. His current net worth was fifty million dollars. His career was starting to take off. However, this was just assets and money. In five years, Tom will probably triple his fortune if he continued on the same pathway.

Tom looked at me with tears in his eyes, and I had no feelings or inclination towards this man. For the first time I questioned myself and hated the fact I was a cold hearted bitch. Why couldn't I feel some sort of sympathy for this man? Why did Havisham create me this way? I felt this conversation had gone on too long, and it needed to end. Tom proceeded to say, "We can discuss the details later. But know I don't want a divorce."

All I could think about was the possibilities of being a single woman. There was no way I would ever fuck him again or pretend to be his wife. I said, "OK Tom, we can deal with this later. I need some sleep. Good night." I was hoping he wouldn't say another word, but he said.

"Estella, can I join you in your bedroom." (We kept separate rooms throughout our marriage). And without turning around, quietly I said.

"No, Tom. Good night." I quickly scurried out of the room, leaving him like a wounded animal.

As I look back on this event, I remembered my inner relief as I finally initiated the closure of that contract. At least that is what I regarded it as. Now some sort of empathetic feelings stirs inside me when I think about that final look Tom gave me.

The next few days, I avoided Tom. I contacted Peter Donovan and arranged what I wanted our divorce proceedings to look like. My flight to New York was scheduled for an early morning, and I thought it would be good decorum to say goodbye to Tom in person. So, the evening before my flight, Felix, our chef, informed me he was in his study. As I approached, I heard him on the phone to his secretary.

"OK, I know. We can move that appointment. And Connie, I'm not sure when I'll be in, so cancel all my appointments for tomorrow afternoon too," Pause, "I know, and when my dad calls. Tell him I'll call him in a few days. Thanks, Con."

I knocked softly, "Sorry for intruding, but I wanted to say goodbye. I'm leaving early in the morning for New York."

Tom, and those wounded eyes that started to tear up again said, "I thought we could talk more about this. We just started, maybe we should try counselling before making any major decisions."

"Tom, there is nothing to discuss. I spoke to Peter yesterday, and he will contact you shortly with all the details. Like I mentioned, there is no going back. Our marriage is done. I'll never forgive you for cheating." At that exact moment I was so thrilled he cheated because that was my out. How could he possibly argue with that? I went over and gave him a hug, then whispered.

"Goodbye, Tom." I left his office strong and resolute. I had a new lease in life, and I knew I crushed the strong, boisterous and dominant Thomas Calloway. I had a flitting thought that Ms. Havisham would be so proud. I was twenty-five; a cold, calculating and controlling woman.

Chapter 3

My takeover of Templeton is proving to be hassle-free; I really do not need to go to the meeting. My team of lawyers is very good and was instructed as to what I want. However, my last sexual contract was over two months ago, and for the life of me I cannot find a replacement.

I'm far from ugly. I know how I look and what I can attract. Plus, I never allow my wealth to dictate who my partner might be. I'm twenty-eight, so I don't need a younger man yet. I tend to go for a bit older. I need educated with a good job, so I tend to go for CEOs, stockbrokers, lawyers and even an FBI agent once. I enjoy the seemingly dominant males because it is rewarding to break them and turn them into submissive. These contracts only last between six months to a year, longer than that they become trite. I never want to remarry, and being a mother is not for me.

I'm five feet seven inches, and I weight 105 lbs. I'm basically tall and skinny with long blond hair, and dark brown eyes. Although my frame is thin, my breasts are perfectly supple. In the North American standards of beauty, I'm a twelve. When I enter a room, people take notice.

My fucked-up childhood was entrenched in wealth and luxury. My benefactor is quite rich and has provided me with the best life has to offer, including my education. I dress with the latest designer fashions (which my personal shopper keeps me in the latest trend), and I own beautiful properties in the US and Europe (mostly acquired after my divorce). Although, I have a driver who drives me in a black escalade, I own about half a dozen top of the line sport cars, and some vintage ones too. I try to drive as much as possible, but I live in Manhattan and I cannot battle the congestion. At home I have a housekeeper, and a personal chef. But for the past couple of years, I cannot bring myself to enjoy food. It's a waste on me, I peck and don't really eat much. My sense of taste has disappeared. I eat a ton of chocolate because I get the faintest taste of sweet from them. I also love the cold; hence why I have not been to my Boca Raton house in a year. I sometimes feel I can't breadth, and cold air helps me to relax.

I have many of psychological issues from my childhood to my teenage years. I did a little counselling during my early twenties, but I felt it was not for me. I am who I am, and I've come to accept it. I will never be that wife or mother who will be devoted to her family. I, simply, cannot love another person. I am selfish and I know some will call me a sadist.

Anyways, I find myself feeling a little joy in the hopes of meeting Mr. Donaldson again. I hate mixing business with my personal life but at this point I'm pulling at straws in the suitable partner department. Plus, I need sex, it has been a little over four months, and I need the release.

My two lawyers who are assigned to this case and I are in the board room. We look domineering and even frightening. Cassandra knocks, then enters and says, "Mr. Donaldson and Mr. Templeton are here." I was not expecting the old man, and I'm a little perturbed that he's here, but I tell Casandra to show them in.

Mr. Donaldson is dressed in a sharp navy-blue suit, and his beautiful green eyes quickly catch mine. I smile to ease the formality, but then glare at Mr. Templeton to ensure he knows I'm not impressed by his presence.

After the formalities of greeting. I commence, "Gentlemen, let's begin. We have all the paperwork here, so this should be quick."

Templeton adds, "My apologies, but if I can interrupt. The final draft removes my daughter as chief editor, as you told Mr. Donaldson to do last week. I would appreciate if you could reconsider this decision. I established this company for her, and this is her baby."

Are you fucking kidding me?! This issue was dealt with and I have given him my decision. Even Mr. Donaldson looks embarrassed.

One of my counsel, Edward Stevenson, responds with, "Mr. Templeton, Ms. Havisham has already given her answer, and I don't believe it has changed." He quickly glances at me, I shake my head. Stevenson continues, "Therefore sir, there is no amendments to this sale."

Donaldson chimes in with, "Mr. Stevenson, my client is appealing to Ms. Havisham's sense of loyalty and compassion. This means a lot to my client, and we would appreciate if Ms. Havisham reconsiders this." He directly addresses that last part to me.

I look him in the eyes and say, "Sir, our offer has been drafted for days, and this sale has already been finalized, so there will be no changes to it." I feel a little sad for old man Templeton and I especially feel bad for Mr. Donaldson, so I add, "Ms. Templeton can stay on for three months, at which time the company will go through a thorough review of its performance, and as the new owner of this company, I will decide who stays and who goes. This is all I'm willing to relent. I will also not be putting this in an amendment, you have my word." I notice Mr. Stevenson shooting me a piecing glance. He knows me well, and this allowance is very unlike my character. I'm a killer when it comes to mergers and acquisitions; I take no prisoners nor allow any favours.

Donaldson seems relatively pleased, but old Templeton knows I'm just postponing the enviable. I need air. Mr. Templeton says, "If there is nothing else I can do, then I'll sign the transfer of ownership to you young lady." He's disappointed and tired, but he's unrealistic. I need to leave, so I say.

"Thank you, Mr. Templeton, my lawyers will take care of the rest. Gentlemen if you will excuse me, I think I am not needed any more." I get up to leave, and say, "Stevenson, you know what to do. Good day gentlemen."

With that I give Mr. Donaldson one last glance and smile, then I take my leave.

He's so hot; all I can think about are those green eyes, supple mouth and broad shoulders. He's not really my type; physically he's gorgeous but his personality is not exactly what I would want to break and crush. He's not a cocky, dominant male. He seems nice and meek, even quiet. He has that bookish type of personality, like a 'do gooder' even. I might be completely off, but I can read people very well (another talent I picked up from Ms. Havisham)—I think he's into me.

As I walk down Broadway and Beaver street, I step into a quaint little eatery, hoping to clear my head of Mr. Donaldson. He's not for me, he's not the type I would go for. He already seems submissive, so what's the point of crushing him? No, he is not the right target. But do I want to hurt him? No. I want sex. I'm craving that sensation. I want to dominate him, tie him up, spank him. Yes, spank him with my black and red flogger. Before I know it, I dial Cassandra, and say, "Get Mr. Donaldson to call, ASAP. Thank you." OK, this might be a little reckless because I don't contact people for personal reasons I do business with. I usually have complete control over my actions, but I feel the desperation of wanting a partner, and he seems to be the man to fulfil that need.

The waitress finally addresses the fact I have not been served. She says, "Sorry about the wait, we are so swamped. What can I get you?" I coldly respond.

"Coffee, and you can bring me the bill; I won't be needing anything else." Her little enthusiastic personality changes to a dull and bored 'OK'. I'm not worth the effort because my order is less than five dollars. This is why I'm indifferent to people. They are selfish beings who only care about what others can give them. This is why I don't need compassion or friends or husbands. Due to my monetary acquisitions and independence, I don't need an emotional relationship with anyone. I am self-sufficient, who does not need a relationship!

My phone buzzes, it's him and I feel nervous, like a stupid schoolgirl. I say, "Hello."

"Hi, Estella. It's James Donaldson. I was asked to return your call. How can I help you?" he sounds friendly and upbeat. I say.

"I'm at Café Regal at Broadway and Beaver, can you come here." There is a pause, and then he says.

"Would you like me to come now?" I respond quickly saying.

"Yes, please." Fuck I sound desperate. Then a little pause and an enthusiastic 'sure' comes out of the phone. I smile and say, "I'll see you soon, goodbye." And I hang up. I get Cassandra on the phone, "Can you move my one-thirty meeting to two-thirty. On second thought, get George to lead today. Tell him I want impeccable notes." I hardly cancel meetings; she must think I went bonkers. She inquires.

"Not a problem. Estella, are you OK? Where are you?" She is so nosy, but she is probably the only person

I would call a friend. I tell her, "I'm fine, just need some air. And I need to meet someone. I have to go, bye." I need to hang up because I don't want her prying now, I'll deal with that in an hour.

Five minutes later, Donaldson steps into the restaurant and all eyes are on him. The hostess, waitresses and patrons are checking him out. He's good-looking. Mind you, people were and are looking at me as well. But I know how to avoid and give cold looks to deter unwanted attention. His office building in literally a block away, I guess this is why my legs took me to this location.

I stand and wave at him, then greet him with, "Hi, thank you for coming. Please sit. What would you like to drink?" He is curious why I called him and why I'm by myself, especially since our meeting just wrapped up about thirty minutes ago.

"Ahh, I'll have a Grolsh, please," he's says to the server, who comes bouncing up to him before he could even sit down. Without paying much attention to her, he continues to me: "I thought today went well."

I say, "No it didn't." And we burst out laughing. He says.

"I know, sorry about that."

"It's not your fault, he should not have been there," I tell him.

He says sheepishly, "Don't blame him, he's a sentimental old man."

That would normally piss me off, but looking at this man puts a smile on my face. So, I change the subject and say, "I don't want to talk shop, tell me about yourself." And right on cue, his beer comes by the bouncing bohemian brunette. He pauses, then says.

"Thank you," and then asks me. "What would you like to know? I enjoy representing old eccentric men," he chuckles. I want to spank him at this exact moment. Instead, I ask.

"Do you enjoy French or Italian wines?"

He responds, "I prefer California. I spent a lot of summers when I went to law school there and I love a nice San Francisco Pinot Grigio." He pauses, then adds, "I honestly don't really like wines, I'm more into beers." Of course, he is. I hate beer, but I don't care about his beverage choices. Cut to the chase, Estella.

He looks at me intensely and says, "You are really intimidating. I mean you are very beautiful, and smart. One of the most successful women in the business industry, so why are you sitting in this little restaurant with me? Don't answer that, I just want bask in your presence." What do I say to this? I am happy he cut to the chase though! He continues, "I mean I want to get to know you, and I'm telling you all this, so you don't think I'm something that I'm not."

"That's an ear full… OK I don't mean to be intimidating. I find you interesting and would like to get to know you." I tell him. I like being honest with everyone and usually I'm quite direct with the people I interact with.

"I find you very attractive and quite interesting myself. I would love to take you to dinner on Friday if you are free?" he asks with a very sweet, boyish voice. In my head all I can think of is no, no... I just want to fuck... you checked out, so fuck me please.

Instead, I tell him, "No dinner, I'll pick you up at your place." He thinks for a second, then says.

"Sure, I'll give you my address. It's four"

"I'll see you around seven on Friday. I have to go to another meeting..." I cut him off as I glance at my watch and stand to leave.

He rises too and says, "Looking forward to Friday then, goodbye Ms. Havisham"

"Mr. Donaldson," and before I could say another word, he plants a kiss on my lips.

"I wanted to do that all day," he explains. I was taken back but it was welcoming. I smile, then exit.

The electricity is uncanny between us!

Chapter 4

On Friday I have a meeting with a potential buyer which is proving to be tedious, so I excuse myself and let my VP, Mr. Darcy, wrap up the meeting.

It's four-thirty, so I head back to my office to review Donaldson's file that my PI compiled. It's a standard procedure I do to all potential interests. I pretty much have everything on him in a matter of a few days including his medical records! I consider the small picture I have of him in his file; he has a strong jaw line, broad shoulders and a beautiful head of hair. He is quite gorgeous. Although his background is clean, I notice he was once engaged... interesting, but this has nothing to do with what I have in mind for him.

In my previous endeavours with these relationships, I don't go on dates or dinners. I don't really want to know these men's motivations, or thoughts. They serve a purpose for me, which includes a distraction from my day-to-day life and a sexual release. Of course, they try to format and build some sort of relationship with me, and usually that's when I terminate the contract with them. I do not tolerate sharing either, so while 'seeing' me, I expect my man to be monogamous. If he dates other women, I end it.

Tonight, I will explain the rules to Donaldson, and before any further proceedings I will have him sign the non-disclosure agreement. It's standard; a girl needs to protect herself. It basically ensures he doesn't discuss this transaction between us with anyone including the media, and whatever I do or we do stays between us. If he breaks the contract, I will then have legal grounds to sue him, and no one wants that!

I pack up around five-thirty because I want to head home to prep for him. The thought of meeting him, and that little kiss gave me a second wind; I feel excited to see him again. His lips were soft and warm, and it still gives me a tingle down in my belly. I clearly needed this, as work is just not enough to cut it right now.

Cassandra is eagerly waiting to see me as well. I don't want to discuss any of this with her at this time, maybe tomorrow. She is good at taking cues. She doesn't push, and that's why I consider her a friend, which is a real rarity in my life. As, I pass her on my way out, she looks at me with her bright eyes and says, "You are leaving early today!" I nonchalantly tell her.

"I'll fill you in tomorrow, I promise." Then I blow her a kiss as I head towards the elevator.

Pierre, my driver and bodyguard, is waiting for me. I tell him the particulars of picking up Donaldson at his place, and the time he will be taken back. All my employees have non-disclosure agreements. No one that works for me can discuss or talk about any business or personal information they acquire while in my service.

I'm excited because he is a little different from who I usually fuck. Although he's not a dominant, which normally turns me on, here I am counting down the minutes for his arrival. I wear a little black dress that is tight and short, which extenuates my tits and ass. It has occurred to me that he might not want what I'm offering. That would be quite disappointing, but men never say no to me, at least not wearing this dress.

The doorbell rings; he's here. I open the door, and he's casually dressed with a tight sweater and jeans. Clearly, he wasn't thinking too formal. He walks up to me and gives me hug.

I still feel the electricity from before. I tell him, "Come in, welcome." As soon as you enter my place, the view of the city is breath taking.

"Wow, you have an amazing view and a huge space, your foyer can hold five of my place," he says while admiring the Manhattan's sky line from my floor to ceiling windows.

I respond, "Thanks, I'll give you a tour later. It's two floors. Would you like something to drink? I have a great 1996 bottle of French Merlot?" He hesitates, then says.

"Sure."

I know he is not a wine drinker, but I like to study people that I have an interest in. My housekeeper, Mrs. Anderson, comes in and takes the order, then exists. Donaldson says, "So a driver and a housekeeper. What other domestic help do you have?" Domestic help? I explain to him.

"It's because I'm really busy with work. I'm never home, and I don't cook. I get a lot of stuff done while I'm in the car too. You can say I optimize my time as much as possible."

Our wines are brought to us. With a slick smile, he says, "Yes, you are very efficient." He takes a sip and literally gags. I almost burst out laughing, but control myself to ask.

"Are you OK? It's a dry wine." He looks a little embarrassed, but says.

"No, it's great." He tries another sip and confesses, "No, it's not. Sorry, it's a bit too dry for me."

I go closer to him and take his glass, then ask, "Wine is not your thing, is it?" He says.

"No, it's not." I tell him in a matter-of-fact tone.

"I have a variety of beers, including Grolsh. Would you like?" Without hesitation he says.

"Absolutely."

I walk into the kitchen and dismiss Mrs. Anderson and Felix, my old chef, for the night. My family room and kitchen are open concept, and tonight I would like some privacy with Mr. Donaldson. I come back with his beer and he says, "You really have an awesome view of Central Park. You work a lot, don't you, so what do you do for fun?"

"That's a good question, and that's why you are here. I seem to have a liking for your company, so let me cut to the chase. I would like you to spend some time with me. A few days a week, nothing too demanding. If you feel the same, then I would like us to be exclusive." I am really not good with the courting or small talk thing because I am direct. He is silent, so I continue awkwardly saying, "I'm a very successful person and somewhat a public figure, so everyone who works for me or is close to me, I insist sign a non-disclosure agreement. Here is the form, I'm sure you are familiar with it. If you want to pursue a relationship with me, then I insist you sign it." I open a folder besides me and hand him the contract. I feel nervous and awkward that this might freak him out and I might have timed all this too quickly.

He peruses it, and then says, "Seems standard." And with that, he took a pen from the table and signs it. I'm a bit shocked by his nonchalant attitude.

"Thanks, that was easy. Do you have any questions about it and have you done this before?" I ask a little in shock by his compliance.

"No and no, I understand why you would have such a contract and I completely agree. You need to protect your interest." He takes a swig of his beer. I'm liking him even more.

"OK, so here is the deal. I don't do the boyfriend/girlfriend thing. I'm too old for that, and don't have the time," I explain. Of course, I don't mention that I don't have the emotional capacity either. "So, what I'm proposing is we keep our contact casual and physical. No relationship bullshit. I never understood those. Of course, I insist if you are seeing me in this capacity you will not date or have a physical relationship with anyone else." I pause to see if he has anything questions, which he doesn't.

"But I do not want an actual relationship that our society has defined for us. I just want your company in a defined physical way. So, no dinners, or actual dating stuff. We can use my place or on occasions yours." I stop because he looks perplex and he's too quiet. I'm nervous that I might have scared him off. I really want this. I really want him.

He finally breaks the silence by saying, "This is different, and kinda strange. So, you just want a sex buddy? Friends with benefits? I might be stupid to say this, but I don't know if that's what I want. I mean I kinda want a relationship with all the bells and whistles, which could potentially go somewhere. At the same time, I can't just end this here. I want more of you." My heart is racing, but his end remarks put me a little at ease. Decent non dominant males are usually not interested in sex with no strings attached. So, it's surprising he's still here.

"I completely understand where you are coming from. But I do really want this with you. I don't know if you are feeling the electricity between us, but I know we would be amazing together. There is no obligations, maybe just try it and see if you like it. I just don't want you to expect more than I can give." I inform him truthfully. OK the ball is in his court, and I feel I need to touch his body, but I restrain myself.

He says, "I can give it a try. I don't know how to act in this scenario or what to do. I can easily be a dick and have sex with you, then leave. I mean any guy would love to do that, but I want to at least know who you are." If that's what it takes, sure I can be civil to him. I tell him.

"I don't want you to get the wrong idea. But sure it doesn't have to be come fuck and then goodbye. We can talk and be civil." This is normally what happens during my contracts, but who knows what he's thinking—at his point I just need him.

"OK we can try. Do we start making love now?" he asks sheepishly. He sounds lost, but cute. What is it about this man that makes me melt?

"We can fuck now," I tell him with a wicked smile on my face. I then slowly walk over to him and start kissing his sumptuous mouth. I wanted to do this the first time I met him. Then I loosen his belt and take off his sweater. His body is toned, he works out. I feel myself getting wet, so I quickly remove his pants.

He says, "This feels so good." I take off my dress. I have a matching black lace bra and panties on. He looks speechless and stunned.

"It feels amazing," I concur. We continue kissing, then I kiss his chest. I want to soak all of him in. His skin feels great beneath my fingers. I take off his boxer briefs and see him swell up in anticipation. He's big and hard. I hold him in my hands and gently stroke him. He kisses me again and cups my breasts in both of his hands. I figure I am going to let him take the lead today. I don't want to freak him out. Right now, I need him to fuck me, however way he wants to.

And fuck, he does... his penis is large and thick. I feel the tip enter, then every single grove of his shaft. He is so big that it initially hurts, but my body adjusts and it becomes a smooth, rhythmic flow. It's magical and he feels so right inside me. As I climax, I hear him moaning and I scream out his name. Shortly after my orgasm, he comes as well with a guttural groan.

I fall asleep on the couch with him. I have not slept with a man in years. I must have been really tired from the day. I check the time to see three-thirty-three a.m. I pull the blanket to cover Mr. Donaldson and myself. I have no energy to crawl into my bed upstairs, and before I know it, I am falling deep into a sleepy maze.

I wake to see these piercing green eyes staring at me. I check the time to see it's eight a.m. Damn it, I've slept in and more embarrassing I slept with him the whole night!

"Good morning, how did you sleep?" I shyly ask.

He retorts, "Good morning, Estella. I slept well. How about you?"

"Not bad, sir. What would you like for breakfast? I'll make something." I say as I pull myself up and notice I am completely naked. I am quite comfortable with my body, so I stand in front of him.

"You!" he yelps. Exactly the response I want. He pulls me onto the couch and begins again to kiss me. I take off his sweater he recently put on and lead him upstairs to my bedroom.

"Can we try something?" I ask a bit nervously.

With a hesitant look, he says, "Sure." I go to my closet and get my handcuffs out, while he sits on the edge on my king size poster bed. When I come out he has a very curious look on his face. I tell him.

"I want to restrain you to the bedrails. Is that OK?" He looks at me then says calmly.

"OK." I proceed to place the handcuffs around his wrists and attach them to my rails. Then I take his pants off, and his penis just springs to life, no boxers to restrict them. I go into my closet and get a brown flogger. When he sees it his eyes widen. "Ummmm, that looks interesting," he tells me.

I reassure him by saying, "It's a flogger and meant to entice pleasure. You will like it. But if you want me to stop, say so and I will." He says.

"OK." So, I brush the ends of the flogger against his chest then down to his penis, stopping there to give it a little lash. He winces but does not protest. I take the flogger to his mouth and lash him on his lips. He winces louder. I brush it across his chest gently, then lash him a little harder across his chest then penis. I lick the strands of the flogger, and then his very hard penis. He gives out a moan. I tell him.

"See, you are liking it. Now close your eyes and just enjoy." He meekly smiles, then complies.

I climb on top of him readjusting myself, so I fit onto his big, hard penis. He still feels tight inside me, but it also feels heavenly. I begin ridding him with the flogger still in hand. As I ride, I caress his body and face with the flogger, and I see him struggling with the handcuffs. I know he's about to come, and I let him find his release. I, too, am building up, and I scream out as I orgasm. "I'm sure we can keep you in good form." I tell him breathlessly as I dismount and lie besides him. I undo the cuffs and he turns to look at me intensely, and asks.

"Is this S and M?" Maybe I have taken it too far for our first time. I really don't want to freak him out. I tell him.

"This is some aspects of it − yes. I am into control; I crave it in both my personal and professional life. The handcuffs I get off on because it restrains you, but the flogger is not just to administer my power over you, it is also meant to yield pleasure for both of us. The pain it creates leads to the threshold of your sexual climax. That's why you came so profoundly!"

This is a lot to digest for him, I am sure, but he smiles and says, "It really was intense. I have never done anything like that before." I ask.

"Really? Not even in college?" He looks at me, then says.

"No, I'm boring!" I laugh and tell him.

"No, you are not. This is the extent of my BDSM. I delve a little into it, but the crazy stuff—like mutilation and extreme pain—I don't really care about. I like restraints, and a little pain." I am watching him intensely to see what he will say next. He looks at me and says.

"My orgasm was very intense, and initially it was outside of my comfort zone, but I enjoyed it." This makes me happy because some men are uncomfortable with this even though it's not quite BDSM. I have a very huge smile on my face when he says this.

I quickly change the topic because I don't want him to change his mind, so I ask, "How about a shower, then some breakfast?" He agrees and I readily take him to my bathroom. I step into the shower and he follows behind. We wash each other's bodies. I have only showered Tom a few times. It feels intimate, but nice. We step out together, and dress ourselves, then head down to my kitchen.

I decide that I will make breakfast today. Plus, I have asked my staff for privacy this morning.

"What would you like? Eggs, toasts, bagels, omelettes, and I'm sure we have bacon." I tell him as I scrutinize the fridge. He seems at ease and content maybe. He says.

"I think I want some eggs, what are you having?"

"I don't really do breakfast, but I need coffee, and maybe a little toast," I tell him in a matter-of-fact tone.

With a perplex look he says, "OK, I'll save the lecture of eating a healthy breakfast for another day, but you should." I have heard this many times! With a more enthusiastic tone, he asks, "What's your plan for today because I would love to go upstate? I know this little town you will absolutely love." Well, I was planning on working and looking over two contracts, but he seems happy, how can I say no? I tell him.

"OK, but I have a few things to do. Pierre can take you home to change and bring you back, and then we can go," he doesn't respond.

As I scramble his eggs, he flips through the New York Times while sitting on the bar stool, and then he casually says, "How about you come with me to my place? Please." I turn and look at him sitting there patiently waiting for his breakfast.

"Sure, but I'll have to take a few calls. Today was going to be a workday for me." I tell him. I'm also curious to see his place.

We eat, I mean he eats his eggs and bread, while I sip my coffee and peruse the financial section of the paper. Then I take him for a tour of my house. I'm very proud of my library as I'm a collector of first edition Victorian novels. Ironically my favourite author is Austen. She creates a world I can never have, so I'm captivated by the unattainable. He likes my Sci-Fi collection of authors like Bell, Gibson etc. My library expands to two floors and one section contains a lot of business periodicals and books, and in a little corner are my classics. I take him upstairs, which has three bedrooms and the luscious primary (which he has seen). Then I show him my main floor and my formal living room, which is an unused space. I keep expensive art pieces in there, such as an original Botticelli, my favourite artist.

We head down to my garage, and today I feel like driving. I show him some of my car collection that includes what I call the shiny collection like my

Lamborghini and Bentley. He gasps, "These are all yours? Wow." I nod and say.

"The whole floor is mine and I like fast things." I choose the Lambo; I need speed today.

Chapter 5

We speed out of the underground garage onto the street. It's a fast car, and of course it's white too. Most of my cars are white. It's a soothing colour that calms me down. I put in his address into my GPS, and he says, "I was going to ask yesterday, but how do you know my address?"

I say with a cheeky smile, "I know a lot about you, Mr. Donaldson. I don't just fuck anyone."

He calmly says, "I wish you wouldn't call what we did fucking. And I know you did your homework on me. When did you know that you wanted me?"

"When I first met you at my office. Did you know I was interested?" I asked.

"No, you came off cold and sterile, very intimidating too. I thought you were mocking me half the time!" he exclaims.

Giggling, I say, "I was not! No not true, I was admiring your physique and handsome face. Daydreaming what I would love to do with you. I hate the city traffic, even on a Saturday. By the way where are we going after your place?"

"We can take my car if you want me to drive. Or I'll put the address into your GPS?" he says.

I tell him, "Put the addy into my GPS" I don't like others driving me, except Pierre, he's ex-military. I hated when Tom would insist on driving. As we pull up to his place, I feel my phone buzzing in my pocket. I wore skinny jeans and a tight nude sweater. I'm not usually casual, but I thought the occasion calls for it.

He leads me up to his house. A good space, a brown stone. The inside is small and typically furnished to suite a single man's need. His furnishing is a bit shabby, but it's impeccably clean. He insists on giving me a tour, which I couldn't resist. At his bed, I start to kiss him. I'm so intoxicated by this man, and my need for his body is incomprehensible. He takes off his clothing and caresses my back, while gently kissing my neck. I snatch his hands and pull him in front of me. I want to fuck hard now.

I undo his pants and start sucking his penis. He swells up in my mouth and he tastes so delicious. I push him unto his bed and take off my jeans and sweater. I know I look hot standing there in my pink lacy bra and panties. I tell him, "I want you now!"

"I want you to come, baby" he says, as I straddle him. "Take it all in. And let me hear you come." he continues. I don't know if I like auditory remarks during sex. I prefer silence, so hopefully he gets the hint from my nonresponse. I start riding him hard, although I'm tight and it hurts. I keep doing it and I feel my build and then that great sensation of reaching my orgasm. As I scream out my release, he comes as well, a deep groan. I fall on top of him and then pull myself on my elbows besides him.

"What are you doing to me?" I ask him with a very pleased look on my face.

He says, "Ms. Havisham I can ask you the same question. You look so beautiful on my bed. But we must go, would you like to take a quick shower with me?"

After the shower, I slip on my casuals and he, too, dress similar with jeans and a sweater, and before you know it, we are on the road again. My Lambo zooms out onto the street and we head for the I-ninety. He already put the addy in my GPS; apparently we are headed somewhere up state. I love taking long rides. Fuck, I forgot to check my phone. I pull it up onto the car system. I would prefer privacy, but that's not an option right now. I check my voice mails, which I have five. I play them out loud on the car's speakers. Two are from Cassandra detailing the stuff I needed to do today, one is from my Japanese client inviting me to a dinner, another from a law office I'm going to be dealing with, but the fifth is from Ms. Havisham! I was about to cut off the voice mail, but she just said it's been a while and she needs to hear from me, happily no mention of my torrid past.

"Incredible, it's not noon yet and already you have that many messages," James says.

I tell him, "I probably got about fifty by now. Cassandra takes all of my office calls and forwards the most important to my cell."

"Cassandra works on Saturday?" he retorts.

Of course, she does, but I tell him, "She does on occasions, it's a busy time right now. So, we are all putting in extra hours. And my employees are highly compensated for their work." *Highly*!

It's a long drive and James is not telling me much about our destination. When we get to this little quaint town, it's so picturesque that I love it right away. The Lambo does not fit in but I park on a quiet street off the main strip. We stroll the downtown core of the town. It's littered with antique bookstores, cute cafes and small restaurants. There is also this beautiful view of a lake that overhangs as the town's back drop.

I, of course, pop into a little bookstore that has that old book smell and grab a copy of Gustave's Madame Bovary. Then James leads me down a narrow alleyway to this cozy little Tuscan inspired restaurant.

As we enter, all heads turn to check us out. I guess we must stand out as tourist to them. "How do you know about this town, this restaurant?" I ask as we settle into a cozy spot in the restaurant.

He responds, "When my family last came to visit me, my sister found the place. The food here is great, and I was told they have a good wine selection too." As he speaks, he looks at me with those kind eyes, which tingles my senses. Although while walking the streets he did not touch me, in here from across the table he holds my hand. This gesture I am not too comfortable with, and he suspects it because he let's go.

Our server comes, James says to me, "Would you mind if I order for you? I think you would love what I choose." I smile and tell him sweetly.

"Sure." I order just a glass of Italian Merlot and James gets a beer.

The food is lovely, simple and rustic. He is right; I love the pasta dish which he ordered me. It is simple and aromatic. When I went to Tuscany I don't think the pasta was this good. But maybe the company is influencing my taste buds today. I almost finish my plate. When the bill comes I insist on paying, but he will have none of it. I inform him that, "This is the 21st century, Mr. Donaldson, you are not required to pay."

He responds with, "I know you are quite independent and wealthy, but I insist." So, I leave it at that.

We stroll the streets once more, then go down to the waterfront. I tell him "Thank you for bringing me here and sharing this with me. It's magical and I love it." Honestly, it is beautiful, and I don't mind that it feels like it's a real date—something I never truly experienced with anyone before, and shockingly this is not freaking me out.

James says, "It was my pleasure. Thank you for coming and sharing this with me." He takes my hand and gently tugs me to him, then kisses me. I feel this electric tingle deep inside me. But I know I need to pull away, this is getting too public and a little emotional. I move away, then head closer to the water. It's a perfect evening; not too cool. There is a gentle breeze coming in from the lake that's refreshing. He stands behind me and I impulsively turn around and hug him, then I peck him on his cheek playfully.

I'm pulled back to reality by my phone buzzing. Fuck I have six missed calls and about twenty emails. I excuse myself and call up Cassandra. I start with, "Hi, I'm fine. I'm not in town... I haven't checked all the emails. Forward the Japanese ones, and the Texas ones to George," pause. "He has instructions on how to handle them... yeah... and message Mr. Yamamtoo's assistant and confirm that I'll attend," pause. "Great, thanks... and that's none of your business. I'm coming in tomorrow. Around noon... no you can stay home." I chuckle. She knows I'm with him and her curiosity is really killing the cat right now.

I look at him, who has a quizzical look on his face, like he knows I'm talking about him. I conclude with, "OK, I think that's it. I'll see you on Monday," pause. "Goodbye, Cassandra." I turn to him and say.

"I'm sorry about that, as I mentioned before I have a lot happening, which I always do. I'm usually better organized, but I wasn't expecting today."

He takes me in his arms, and says, "It's my fault. I'm sorry, how can I help?" He seems earnest, but I feel uncomfortable now because we are in public. I pull away and say.

"Let's head back."

We walk silently to the car and I open the door for him and with a cheeky remark I say, "See, chivalry isn't dead." And with an irresistible wink to go along with it.

He retorts with, "Some might say you are emasculating me, but I'm enjoying your independence."

It is already evening as I drive us back to his place, I want more but I have work to do. Of course, he says, "I might be able to rustle up a bottle of wine, can I get you to come up?"

"I need to deal with a few things, but just a quick drink," I tell him defeated. I want more and I want to feel him inside me. We go up, and he has a nasty, cheap bottle of Rose. I decline but get him to pour me a Scotch. He's surprised that I want hard liquor but I need a drink. I feel the need to say, "I don't normally drink hard liquor, but I need something to calm me down. Today was not what I was expecting."

He says, "What were you expecting?"

What was I *expecting*? Not spending the whole day with him in a beautiful, magical place, that's for sure. I say, "Sex, then a goodbye." And I give him my biggest smile. We both giggle.

I sip my drink and then go over to him by his island in his kitchen. We start kissing and undressing each other. He leads me to his couch and starts kissing my belly and tits. He goes past my belly button onto my clit. It feels heavenly. He then kisses my thighs in a teasingly sort of way. I want his tongue inside me. "Put your tongue inside," I command, and he obeys. In and out he goes. Then he sticks two fingers inside me. I'm so wet. I start to move against his fingers. I feel myself building—faster and faster, and I start screaming as I come. I want his penis inside me right away as I orgasm. "Put your penis inside me, now," I order, and he obliges. He starts going fast and hard. It feels amazing, and I feel him building and he comes whispering my name.

We must have fallen asleep as we are still on his couch when I glanced at his golf clock on his mantle. It's three-thirty-three a.m. I slip away and gather my clothing. I quickly change, then head downstairs to my car.

Chapter 6

What am I doing? This is what the norms call dating! I'm too old and tired for this. I need to cut him loose because he's clearly pushing for more and I'm allowing it. I need absolute control on this contract or I'm going to end it. I don't do boyfriends or relationship, and this feels too much like that. I mean after our first night of fucking, I allowed him to take me on a road trip with dinner, shopping and a breath talking view! What am I doing with this guy?

I'm in my bed and I can't go back to sleep. My mind is racing and there is so many things that I am thinking of—work, James, Havisham etc. Sleep is eluding me, so I go to my office at home and try to be productive.

Three hours later, it's ten a.m. and already I got all my emails sorted. James has called twice and left one message, which I can't bring myself to check yet. I need to grab control of this situation before I have any interaction with him.

Since Tom, I had sexual relationships with three other men, then ended the relationships when they became trite or did not suite to my liking. One lasted eleven months but he wanted more, and I knew he fell in love with me. It was not pleasurable ending it with him because the sex was good, and we had good conversations. I ended the contract by calling him on the phone, and I told him that I didn't feel the same and it was just sex. So, I didn't think it should continue; he was crushed and pleaded to continue seeing me. I hung up.

The other long one was seven months. He was my age and too immature, but great in bed. I let it go on that long because he understood I could not have any other relationship with him. He was perfect because he would come over, fuck and leave. We shared nothing in common and no need to chit chat. Although that sounded perfect on paper, I became bored by the sex, so when that went there was nothing left. The other one was short. I didn't like his personality per say. But he allowed me to dominate him, and I outlined the sex. He eventually wanted more like dates and dinners etc. and of course that is not my scene.

Now Mr. Donaldson has come into my life. He's very different from the rest. He's not cocky or dominant. He's reserve and humble. He's kind, and like I initially thought, for lack of a better phrase, he is a 'do gooder'. He reminds me of my first male interest, Philip. They both have that nice guy persona. That's not what I'm accustomed to because I never really pursued Philip. I enjoy breaking down tough and controlling men. So, what am I supposed to do with him? What is there to break down?

This is new territory for me, and I'll admit that it did feel good spending yesterday with him, but is that what I want? No, he will leave me eventually, so I cannot be emotionally tied to him. My heart has never been awoken and therefore has never been broken. I do not want to change that. If I cannot remove all feelings from my interactions with Mr. Donaldson, then I need to break it off.

I ignore his two calls and his message which I finally check, and it reads: 'I had a great time yesterday, but I wanted to make you breakfast. I know you are busy, call me when you can'. I like it because it's not pushy, although I don't respond. I need to think and do some work to clear my head.

Another thing that's been eating away at me is Ms. Havisham's message. She wants me to call her. I haven't spoken to her in a while, so it was strange to get a call from her. Our relationship has become estranged after I left Tom. Although she was overjoyed that I absolutely crushed that man, I was not happy about it, more indifferent to it. She thought the marriage went on too long and wanted me to end it before. I usually do whatever she wants, however, I have evolved from her tyranny.

When I was a teenager, she would control all the boys I interacted with, and she even hand selected Tom as my fiancé. I did what she bid me to do without hesitation. Her happiness was important to me, and her hatred of love seeped into my soul, but manifested itself not so much as hate, but as love's non-existence.

She embedded into me a strong distaste for marriage and relationships. From her teachings, I truly believe men are not capable of monogamy or love, therefore I will never allow myself to be that foolish to fall 'in love' with anyone. Instead, I manipulate them to 'love' me then I leave them. I think now I don't care for them to love me any more; I just want good sex.

Ms. Havisham, when she was younger allowed herself to foolishly fall in love with some young man that only wanted her wealth. When he found out her family was insisting on a prenup, he left her at the alter in front of 150 people. It was reported that she was so embarrassed and heartbroken that she locked herself in her room for five days and did not leave her parents' home for a year, and only wore her wedding dress during that time. It was also rumoured that she attempted suicide twice.

She never got over the embarrassment and from that stemmed her hatred for all men. After her parents died, they left all their wealth and the Havisham's Real Estate Development company to her. Adela's father cut out the second child, Arthur, from his will because as a teenager they had a falling out (he is Adela's half-brother). I don't know the particulars, but Adela was always the old man's favourite. Her tragedy only reinforced that he needed to protect her, so she inherited everything.

She still runs the real estate company, but in a secondary sort of way. I have overseen the company for the past eight years.

One day I guess she was bored and wanted a companion, so she adopted me… or so she told me.

During my last year of marriage with Tom, I became curious and wanted to know more about my birthday mother. So, my PI did some digging. It took him months to reveal that I'm a Havisham by blood. Apparently, my mother was none other than Arthur's daughter. I always envisioned a crack whore giving birth to me, but that crack whore turned out to be Adela's niece. She knew and never told me about my birth mother—that broke my heart.

My so-called mother was Arthur's eldest daughter, Christina. She had a turbulent relationship with her parents and ran away at sixteen. She was addicted to cocaine and heroin and got pregnant. She died during childbirth. I bounced around for a couple of months in foster care, until Adela found and took me in as her ward. Don't confuse the idea of a mother and a benefactor. There is not one motherly instinct in Adela—I was just her ward.

I don't know who my father is. I really don't care either, but I don't like surprises, so Peter (my PI), is still digging.

The fact that I'm a Havisham doesn't mean much to me. I don't care that I am related to this fucked up family. I want nothing to do with my 'grandfather' either. What does hurt is that Adela never told me any of this. She led me to believe that my mother was a junkie that overdosed, which is technically true, but she always claimed that she does not know who my mother was.

I felt betrayed when I found out three years ago, and as a result I distanced myself from Adela. Initially, she called many times, and even came to my house in New Hampshire. But I refused to see her and after a while the phone calls dissipated.

This information and the breakdown of my relationship with Adela hit me hard. I guess it propelled me to end my marriage with Tom, become independent and move to New York. But I still manage her real estate development company.

So, this phone call is disconcerting since I have not heard from her in thirteen months. She sounded urgent and needy. This is very unlike the strong and commanding Adela that raised me. I still don't want to see or speak to her. I can forgive her for the fucked-up way she raised me, but the least she could have done was tell me the truth about my family.

***

It's already midday, and all I want to do is crawl into bed and think about James. But I decide that I need time to process everything. I can't forget myself because some good-looking man just so happens to also be great in bed. I need to keep him at arm's length.

I get what I want to get done today, and then decide to call up Cassandra. As the phone rings, I think about the arrangements that she must work on this week for me, and I also need to give her other directions on some initiatives I have brewing. To be honest, I also want to explain my behaviour to her.

"Hi, Cassandra," I say, a little flustered. "I hope that I didn't catch you at a bad time. But I wanted to talk to you about the Japanese investment and booking that party for me."

Cassandra responds with, "Hi Estella, should I come over?"

I tell her, "No its Sunday." Fuck it, I'll just tell her: "Actually I can text you the details, but what I want to say is I met up with Donaldson the other day, after our meeting." A slight pause, then she says.

"I figured you did, what's going on? Are you interested in that person?"

I say, "Yes, I am. We are kinda seeing each other in my sort of way." She knows some aspect of my life, and she is aware that I cannot committee.

She continues with, "Ahh, I see. Well, he seems like a decent sort of fellow. Estella, I know you can take care of yourself, but it is OK to let down your guard sometimes." What is she getting at!

I quickly tell her, "Thanks for the advice. I'll message you the details. See you tomorrow." With that I hang up. She will understand that the last part of her speech was unnecessary.

***

I can hardly get anything done! I want to call him so badly… I wrap up my calls and get myself dressed. I call Pierre to get the car ready. As I sit in the SUV, I have an urgent need to see James. I know I shouldn't, not yet, but I tell Pierre to take me to his home.

I message him that I am downstairs and literally in two minutes he's outside helping Pierre to open my door. "Hi," I greet him. He looks good.

He responds with, "Hi it's freezing, come on in. Where is your coat?" Ohh, I didn't realize I wasn't wearing a coat.

I tell him, "I must have left it at home."

He takes me inside. I feel hot, sweaty even. It's two degrees outside, but my blood is pumping through my veins and my ears are hot. He wraps his arms around me, and whispers, "Can I make you some coffee, tea, oh and I bought new wine!" He thought I would come back to him, and when did he have time to buy new wine? And more importantly, am I becoming that predictable?

"I am sorry I didn't respond to your message; I was really tied up with work." I say as I pull away from him. "But I got everything done." He smiles and stares at me with those piercing green eyes.

"It's OK, I figured you were busy. I had a really good time yesterday," he tells me.

I walk over to his kitchen and examine the chardonnay that he bought, it's decent. He follows me with his eyes, and comments, "It was the most expensive bottle at the liquor store around the corner. I figured it must be somewhat good?"

I say, "It's not bad, a bit dry but good. Would you like to join me for dinner? We can either go out or I can have Mrs. Anderson prepare us something." He contemplates, then says.

"Or we can stay here. We can order in? Or I can make us something?"

I ask to open his fridge, then quickly say, "This will not do. Let's order in." Staying at his place will have its advantage of me leaving at any time.

Plus, I need to clear my head of Ms. Havisham. He makes food suggestions, but I'm thinking or trying to figure out if I'm going to call her back. Previously, I have not returned her last eight calls, but something about her voice makes me think she needs me.

He's asking something. "Sure," I respond. And he says.

"Chinese it is then. Are you all right? You seem millions of miles away, want to talk about it?"

I say, "Not really, just need to deal with my benefactor. I don't know if I should call her." Fuck I said too much.

He asks, "You mean Ms. Havisham, your adopted mother? I Googled you. Why won't you call her back?" Because she committed child abuse and lied about my birth mother.

I say instead, "She was the farthest thing from a mother. And it's complicated. Anyways, do you have a menu, or we can pull it up on my phone. I don't eat much, so just order what you want. I'll peck." He comes over and hugs me, then kisses my cheek. I ask, "What's that for?" He tells me.

"Because you came back and you are going to eat greasy Chinese food with me!" This puts me into a better mood.

A few hours later, as we eat our takeout Chinese food, I notice his sketch pad, and flip through it without asking. He's talented, but I could tell he is hesitant of me looking at it. I don't think he wanted me to see it. That doesn't stop me from asking, "These are good. Really good, why are you hiding them?" They are mostly nature images, but beautiful shading and oil colours. I'm impressed; I didn't see this side to him.

He shyly says, "Thanks, it's just a hobby, nothing special. I like driving out of the city to find inspiring landscapes. I was thinking of doing a piece on the lake we walked down to." He stops and looks a little embarrass. I reassure him.

"You are very talented, and that lake would make a great piece for a painting. You should definitely do it."

We talk into the late evening, then I take my leave without sex. I feel happy, content even. This is a mystical and new sort of territory for me. I don't know how comfortable I am about it though, but I don't want to overthink it.

I am looking forward to work tomorrow as it will keep me grounded and thankfully occupied.

Chapter 7

The next day, around ten a.m. I resolve to call her. I might as well, she's been on my mind since Saturday. Earlier James messaged me, but I didn't respond. He wants to see me again soon, but I need some distance from him and these feelings. I don't know what to make of them, plus this Havisham matter is on my mind right now.

I pick up the phone and dial. On the third ring, Berta, the housekeeper answers. "Hi Berta, it's me. How are you?" She has always been kind to me, and her warmth was so infectious in a very cold house when I was young.

"Ms. E, is that really you. Ohh, we have missed you so much. When are you coming home?" That's a strange question, I ask her.

"I'm good. What's wrong, Berta? Is everything OK?"

There is a pause, then she says, "I better let you talk to Ms. Havisham." And with that she is gone. After an eternity it seems, a weak, feeble voice greets me on the phone.

"Estella, is that you?" Adela asks.

She sounds helpless, I say, "Yes Adela, I got your message. How can I help you?"

She says, "I called because I haven't heard from you in a long time, and I wanted to make sure you were OK."

She pauses, "And since you are my power of attorney I wanted you to know I had a minor stroke." I gasp, why didn't someone contact me right away?

"*What*? When did this happen? Why wasn't I told? Are you OK? Adela speak to me please!" I plead. After a pause, she says.

"I didn't know if you would care, and I didn't want to bother you. It happened about a month ago."

I feel my blood boiling inside me, and I couldn't help it but I start screaming into the phone: "Why would I not care Adela! I have lived with you longer than anyone. Of course, I care. You should have called earlier."

I paused to take a breath. Then with a very controlled and even quiet voice, she says, "Estella, you have no right getting angry with me. You stopped taking my calls three years ago. So, you have no right to be mad at me." She is right, she doesn't owe me anything. I tell her I'll be home soon. She says in very controlled and quiet voice, "Good," then hangs up.

This is agonizing. I call Pierre and have him arrange to get a small bag packed for me, and to get my private jet ready for a departure tonight. I'll spend Tuesday and some of Wednesday with her, then head back by Wednesday night.

I wrap things up in the office by telling Cassandra my plans. I tell her that I'll do a video conference from New Hampshire and take a few important calls, the rest she can forward to Mr. Darcy. I call Darcy and tell him the urgent matters that he needs to deal with in my absence. Since the last pandemic, work now is easy to get done remotely.

With regards to James, I message him that I'll be in New Hampshire because something important came up with Ms. Havisham, but I should be back soon. Literally a minute later, my phone buzzes, and James is on the other end. I say, "Hi, you got my message?"

He responds by saying, "Yes, I hope everything is OK, what can I do?" He sounds genuinely concerned.

"Nothing I'll be back soon; Adela just had a minor stroke and I want to make sure she is OK. Thanks for calling," I say.

He tells me, "Estella, of course. If you want me to be there with you, just say the word. I'm here for you." That's quite the gesture since I barely know him.

"Thanks, James. But I'm sure I can manage. I'll message you when I get back. Bye," I tell him, cutting off the conversation. I am a little taken back by his gesture to come with me. That's way too serious, and I need some distance from him. He's too intense and makes me feel out of my norm.

I put him aside in my head and pack some work for the trip. Pierre comes and help me to the car; he accompanies me on all my trips. Within an hour we are in the sky on our way to New Hampshire: the Havisham's estate.

***

It's a grand property, with a large Victorian house that is about 18000 square feet. The property is about fifteen acres, with ponds and meadows. It has a large fitness court that I played tennis on with my trainer when I was a teenager. It also has a cascading waterfall the leads to an Olympic size pool. On the far-left side sits two guest houses that are self-contained. I thought we lived in a castle when I was going up. The estate has a full staff, from two butlers, three cooks and several house maids. And of course, Berta. She has been with the Havishams for two generations.

As we approach the gates, Pierre calls into the monitor and the rod iron gate opens. Pierre drives straight through up to the roundabout front entrance. Although I still have my keys, I go up to the front doors and ring the doorbell. A middle-aged woman opens the door, I don't recognize her but she is expecting me. She says, "Ms. Havisham please come in." She has a Swedish accent. Adela always changes up her help. She hates keeping them long term because she is always suspicious that what they hear and see might become public knowledge, despite the confidentiality agreements they signed. The only resilient person to withstand her is Berta.

The blond woman scuffles off and leaves me in the formal foyer. I remove my coat and place it in the nearby closet. I then head into the living room and was about to make my way into the kitchen, when Berta comes bouncing in. I run to her and throw my arms around her big shoulders. She feels so warm and comfortable. Tears start streaming down my cheeks, I did not realize how much I've missed this woman. She comforts me by saying, "My baby, don't cry. I'm here. You are home, and you will be fine. Berta is here for you, my babe." I give a sob then kiss her on the cheek and say, "I've missed you so much." I never cry, so this is shocking and new to me. At this moment I feel exhausted and just want to sleep.

I ask, "Where is she?" Berta explains.

"Ms. Havisham stays in her room most days. Hardly comes out and refuses to meet any callers. She is ill and doesn't want to get any help. Estella, you have to go see her and fix her. She misses you so much. All she wants to do is talk about you. She gets me to hunt down all the magazines you are in and news articles. I show her your pictures and we read about your life. That makes her happy."

This hurts me because I'm not there for her, but she hurt me too. I tell Berta to take care of Pierre and that I'll be staying in my old room. Then I go upstairs to unpack.

I am eager to meet with Adela, but Berta says she just went for a nap. So, I decide to explore my childhood home. I head into the dining room. It's grand with mahogany, baroque style wood wainscoting throughout. The table holds twenty chairs comfortably. Adela had her ladies social club meetings here sometimes, or a dinner ball would start here. It's a beautiful room, with Renaissance artwork along two walls. I thought this room was so grand when I was a child. I take a seat at the head of the table and look across the room. What Adela has done to me is unforgiveable, but she did take me in, and showed me some sort of compassion over the years.

It's already five p.m. so I find a housekeeper and tell her what I want for supper. I have made up my mind that when Adela is ready to see me, she can come and find me. I then glide through some more rooms in the house, while I reminisce about what happened during my life in each of these rooms. I head into a formal living room that has Persian tapestries and antique furniture. In earlier days this was such a great room, however, it is now a bit dated and old. I remember pretending to be a Persian princess and the tapestries were my magic carpets. Now the room needs an overhaul. I bet Adela has not step foot into this room for over ten years. I then walk into a smaller drawing room. I remember as a child I would sit by the piano and play a piece, while Adela read or crocheted.

Promptly at seven p.m. Chrissy (the blond, Swedish woman), informs me that dinner is ready. I take my place in the dining room, and she comes in with a chicken salad and a glass of chardonnay. Halfway through my meal Ms. Havisham joins me. She has a walking stick for support, and I cannot help but think how feeble and old she looks.

"Hello, Adela. I'm here as I promised. You don't look very well. Can you please tell me what happened?" I ask her in a stern and cold tone, without getting up.

She starts with, "Estella, I have not seen you in a long time. You look wise and if possible angrier." She gives out a chuckle, but I'm not amused. She sits and continues, "I miss you a lot, but I'm sure Berta has already told you that." She pauses then adds, "I've grown quite old since you last saw me and sickly. I guess that comes with age." She stops. She seems unhappy and depressed.

"I'm sorry you are sickly." I say awkwardly, not knowing what to say. I continue, "Have you eaten today?"

She tells me, "No, I can't think of food." I look at her then call for Chrissy, who comes in and turns red at the sight of Adela.

"Can you get Adela some food and a glass of milk, thanks?" I ask. Adela stares at me blankly, and I say, "If you are not going to take care of yourself, then I guess I'll have to. I wish you or someone called me earlier!" There is silence then Adela snaps.

"You left me and never returned. Why would anyone call you?" She is livid, so I snap back.

"You lied to me."

"What are you talking about?" she innocently asks.

I am done holding back (she doesn't know I know), so I retort, "My birth mother, you knew who she was yet told me she was some unknown junkie. But that junkie was your niece, wasn't she?" I use my ace; end of story Adela, you lose.

She turns white, then quietly says, "I knew one day you would find out. She was my niece, and I didn't tell you. So what? What does that matter? Did you want my brother to be your grandfather and guardian? I thought I did you a favour keeping you away from them!"

I never thought about, Arthur, Adela's brother and my supposedly grandfather. I never liked that man, and neither did Adela. I say earnestly, "I don't care where my mother came from, but I trusted you and I assumed you would always tell me the truth. I devoted my life to pleasing you, and you simply betrayed me." I cannot forgive her for that.

She says, "I did you a favour, you are a better person because you did not think of Arthur as family, and you knew how to be independent without relying on the Havisham's name. You didn't really identify with it and trust me that made you a stronger and more successful woman. That's all I'll say on that subject. I do not regret keeping it from you either," she stops. Her words have conviction and I know she means all of it, and there will be no sense changing her mind to my version of betrayal.

"I don't like being lied to," I said sounding like a sulky child. I continue drinking my chardonnay and Adela says.

"You have attained a lot of success with your company. Berta and I read about it almost every day. How's Tom?" that's a change of subject.

"My company is my baby. I'm quite proud of it. As for Tom, the last time I saw him was at the house in Hanover, about three years ago. He did not protest the divorce, and all of this you are aware of." I stop myself, I'm still angry at this woman.

She continues, "How have you filled the void of Tom? Did you get another submissive?" Wow, she doesn't miss a beat. She is so feeble, yet she is still interested in my sex life! What a woman. I don't really want to talk to her about James. I don't even know what I have with James. But I say.

"Not exactly a sub, but I am seeing someone. Adela I'm tired, can we continue tomorrow?" She stares at me with her icy blue eyes and says.

"Sure." Adela's food comes and then we chat about what happened to her in the last three years.

Chapter 8

Sleep eludes me in my old childhood bed. Adela keeps haunting my thoughts. She is pulling me back into her life. I have forgiven her about my mother, but since leaving her three years ago, I come to realize the abuse she has inflected upon me. To put it simply, she has fucked me up completely. I don't trust anyone, I don't believe in love, I want to physically and emotionally hurt men, I would never completely trust anyone—and this is all thanks to Adela! She has brainwashed her believes onto me since she became my benefactor. I have come to realize that going to all the brothels and the mind games she made me play with Philip, the other boys and then Tom were a form of child abuse. Instead of turning out to be a normal human being, I'm a lonely fucked up woman who's incapable of love.

What should I do? I can't abandon her like I did for three years. She will surely die, but I can't let her control me. She is right—if Arthur was to know I was his granddaughter my life would be miserable-like his children. I shudder at the thought.

I cannot sleep, instead I admire the sun rise from a bay window that overlooks a huge pond lined with weeping willows. It's a beautiful spring morning, so I decide to shower and go for a walk around the grounds. I can smell the trees and water in the air as I stroll around the pond. I sit underneath a huge willow tree and admire the garden I am in. I remember the countless summer days I spent at this exact spot, reading, and writing my stories. I get lost in my reverie, but I am able to clear my head and come up with a plan. I decide it is time to head back in.

Upon my return, Berta has my coffee ready and the papers. I give her a big hug and tell her I'll be staying for a bit longer. She is elated. I go to Ms. Havisham's room to tell her I'll be staying for a while but will be commuting to New York for work. She offers up her company's jet, in which I decline, citing that I'll use my own.

***

I spend the next month with my benefactor. I am good for her health, and she is good for mine as she makes me focus on work and in essence thawing any sort of 'feelings'" I felt for James. He messaged me many times during the first two weeks and called a few times. Now once or twice a week he would message saying, "I hope you are well. I am always thinking about you." I do not respond to these messages because I don't know what to tell him. I cannot lie to him, and I feel if we spoke I would tell him how I feel about him—which is a bad idea and he will surely reject me.

I thought I escaped Ms. Havisham's curiosity on the topic. But one afternoon, when we are having tea she asks, "You mentioned you were seeing someone. Who is he?"

I respond saying, "He's of no consequence. I don't plan on seeing him again."

She asks, "Why not? He's a man, I'm sure you would like to turn him into your sub?" I feel gross now when she talks about my sexual relationships like this. I tell her.

"He's not a dom to begin with. He's just a nice guy. He was a mistake."

"They are all pigs, Estella—all of them. None of them would ever care for you. Don't you forget that. This mystery man is not a nice guy, I am sure he broke some stupid girl's heart and if he didn't, he will. You should crush him, Estella." Ahh, back to the old life. No, I don't want to crush James, I just want him far away from me, so I don't hurt him or him to me.

I say sternly, "He's not my type, Adela. End of story. I need to go home next week. You are feeling better and looking well. And I have quite a few things I need to attend to in New York. Plus, I need to go to Seattle to Havisham Inc. That vice president you appointed has fucked up two buildings slotted for office units in California. I need to go on Friday to meet with your investors and fix the problems." I shouldn't have to deal with this issue because she should not have hired this new vice-president without my consent; granted I wasn't talking to her, but nonetheless I must fix his fuck up now.

I see the worry look in her old, wrinkled face, she then says, "Can't you come back here when you are done in New York?" Translation, can't you live here?

"Adela, I have a home and a thriving business. I need to go back. But you can come visit me anytime." I tell her with a soft tone. That should suffice, but she looks downcast. I quickly move on saying, "I am thinking of attending a charity art auction in Chicago this weekend, would you like to join me?" This should cheer her up, but I know she wouldn't come—she doesn't leave her house now. The truth is for the last month I have been flying into New York once a week, and basically overseeing everything from Adela's drawing room. Although it is working, I need to be there full time, actually I don't, but I don't want to stay here. I miss my independence.

For the next couple of days, we converse and reconnect about what has happened in our lives. I don't ever mention James and she knows I'm avoiding him. Although she doesn't even know his name, because of my coy avoidance of him, she knows something is up. I don't know what it is about this woman, but she really gets to me.

During the month of being in the same house with her, all my old thoughts and feelings resurfaced. I see the world with Ms. Havisham's lens. The world is a cold, heartless place and all men are disgusting pigs. She has placed her putrid outlook of the world into my skin again. I was never a warm or fuzzy person, but I thought after I ended the marriage with Tom, I became a little softer and not so negative because I ultimately crushed a strong man. I knew I was fucked and was willing to possibly change a few things about myself. James, I felt, might have been good for me; he brought out a lighter side to me I didn't know I had.

But thanks to Adela, whatever flicker of hope of changing myself or finding a normal relationship has dissipated. My life seems to be back to the idea of inflicting pain onto any man who are stupid enough to fall in love with me. I need to go home and distance myself from her. She is suffocating me; I need out of this house.

***

The Friday before I plan to head home, I go to Seattle to deal with Adela's development company. When I walk into the office, everyone is expecting me. I assume Adela told her people I was coming. I schedule a meeting with the vice president, but instead Adela arranged a meeting with the whole board. I am not prepared for this, but I can handle it. I wish she would communicate better with me.

As I walk in all eyes are on me, I greet them with a smiling, "Good morning."

Simultaneously, they all say good morning. Then I ask Mr. Bill Weaver, senior vice president, "What do I owe this pleasure for all of you being here?" Mr. Weaver, with a pretentious smile, says.

"Congratulations, Ms. Havisham you are now majority shareholder and CEO of Havisham's Real-estate

Development Company." I look at them with shock, and disbelief. Fuck of course, Adela made me CEO! This is insane, and a bit too much even for her. I step back, wanting to leave the room. But I realize they are all staring and waiting for me to say something.

I burn up, I need air, but that will have to wait. I quickly fumble and say, "Wow, sorry I wasn't expecting this. Ms. Havisham's did not mention this to me. Umm, it's a huge honour and I will need some time to digest this before I give out an official statement. But let me say, this company has always been near and dear to me. And as you all know I have been overseeing all operations for the past ten years, so I am up to speed. I am looking forward to working personally with each and every one of you and to continue to make this company thrive for us all. Thank you." Everyone applauds.

People come up to congratulate me, I feel the *fakeness* of their smiles and well wishes. I quickly shake their hands and thank them politely, then I find an exit. I message Pierre, and he's leading me to the elevator in a flash. I dial up Adela as soon as we exit the building.

"What is the meaning of this? Are you insane? You want me to run your company? Why didn't you warn me this morning?" I say frantically, then I stop. I'm panicking because she is trapping me into her world again.

She says, "Estella, we will discuss when you get home," and she hangs up without saying anything further.

I tell Pierre to drop me off at a small park we saw on the way in. I need some time to think before I board the jet.

I take a seat on a park bench, and just stare into space, with a million things rushing into my head. I know I was her heiress because she has no one else to bestow her money, property or company to. She thinks her brother is a manipulating idiot, and her niece and nephew are fools. They were very nasty to me growing up as they always treated me like an outsider—a dirty orphan. They never played with me.

As a teenager, I was accomplished and beautiful, so of course Arthur's son wanted to make friends, and his daughter was jealous. I ignored them, and thankfully Adela wanted nothing to do with them either. Needless to say, I really was their niece this whole time, but I don't think that would have changed anything.

I need to deal with this. It was inevitable because at some point I was going to get this company. I thought after our rift, she might have reconnected with Arthur or one of his kids or grand kids (I think he has three of those), but I guess that was not the case.

This company has been a part of 'our' family for generations. It established the Havishams as American royalties back in the fifties. One of the biggest and established real estate development companies in the US. They are a trusted name, with a successful repertoire. Adela ran the company, but for the past fifteen years she oversaw all major decisions from her home. She hired trusted people to run the day-to-day mechanics. I was assisting her for the past ten years by checking up on the accounts, projects and her management teams.

If I take on this role, I will have to overhaul a few of the senior management and base a lot of the mechanics of this company in New York. It should have been in New York to begin with. This company is stagnant over the last two years because of Mr. Weaver's incompetence. I have recently told Adela this, but she has no one to replace him. With a proper VP, this company can fly! OK, so I can manage it if I can run the logistics from New York. I'll keep the massive tower in Seattle, and my communications company can be within this umbrella. I have done this before many times when I acquire new companies. It's not that difficult, but you need the right team. I do understand that this will be the biggest company I would have… and everything else will be a secondary thought.

Suddenly, I think of James as a bird flit off the bench next to me. I miss him. He's been at the back of my mind for the past few weeks. His messages have dwindled, but he's still in my head. I yearn to see him and feel his touch.

I make my way back to the car. Pierre is waiting for me; we go to the tarmac and within an hour I'm back at Havisham's estate.

Adela and I are having a tete a tete in her room. Before I tell her my plan, she explains in her controlled, poised voice: "Estella, the company and everything I own has always been yours. But you are so stubborn, you ran off to New York without consulting with me, and formed that telecommunication company. Why telecommunication? I don't know, but you have proven yourself to be a shrewd businesswoman, who doesn't rely on other people's handouts. I can respect that." Good!

After graduating college, I didn't want to rely on or be controlled by either Tom or Adela. I wanted to establish my own legacy, but they both helped me with their cheque books. She continues, "You have always taken care of Havisham's development, so I'm not worried. You are very smart and very business savoy. I invested a lot of money in your education, so I know for a fact you can do this." I commence to say.

"I know I can, but I'll run it from New York." I know she doesn't want to hear this, but oh well. I communicate my plans of putting my company under the development company and running it like that. I know she wants all of my attention on her family's company that they have created and own for over sixty years, but I cannot just drop what I have worked so hard to accomplish, and she knows this. I know she isn't quite happy with this plan, but she knows I'm too stubborn to budge at this point.

She concedes and frowns. To sooth her, I tell her again she can come visit me at any time in New York. Her estate lawyer will contact my lawyers with the details tomorrow and the transfer of ownership documentation will need to be signed soon after. A thought pops into my head, which is to have James as my advising lawyer, but I cannot mix business with pleasure, plus if Adela meets him, she'll have him for breakfast.

After my meeting with Adela, I head up to my room to pack. Strangely I miss James! Even though I don't really know much about him, I feel I have known him for a long time. He has that sort of warmth that I lack, but apparently crave. Alas, it's been over a month, and I'm sure he has moved on.

Chapter 9

It's time to say my goodbyes to the staff and of course my dear benefactor Ms. Havisham. I want our goodbyes to be brief and quick. I go to her room, and quietly slip in. She is sitting by the window combing her long hair, while staring out into the beautiful, manicured garden.

I startle her by saying, "Adela, I'm packed, and I'll be leaving shortly. I'm here to say goodbye and thank you for letting me stay here. Oh and of course, giving me the sole ownership of your mega company!" I say this with sarcasm and a funny intonation, but I think Ms. Havisham has missed the cue.

She says, "Estella, I don't want you to go, but I know I can't do anything to keep you here. I will miss you. I'm a lonely old lady, and you were to be my companion, but I think I made a too independent prodigy, so for now I will recede. But don't you ever forget what I've taught you. Do not trust anyone, especially men. They will hurt you if you ever do." How could I possibly forget these life lessons when they are engraved in my soul? Of course, these memories and lessons of my childhood and adult life will always be a part of me.

I awkwardly go over to hug and kiss this frail, old woman. I tell her to take care of herself and I'll come visit soon. She hugs me back. As I leave the room, I feel a weird pang in my chest because I know she is the closest thing I have to a mother. Her frailty and that sad look on her face will forever haunt me.

Pierre is waiting for me at the door to take my bags to the car. Before I head out, I seek out Berta to give her a big hug and kiss, and make her promise that she will call if anything comes up.

***

Back in my comfy, private home, I plan my return to the office tomorrow and I message Cassandra to come over with a few things I can sign off on to ease my day. Plus, I want to know everything that happened in my absence.

In two hours she is at my door. She hugs me, which takes me back. I tell her, "Hi to you too, I only saw you last week!"

She says, "I thought you would never come back!" I chuckle at this because if could have very well been true. Then she asks if I have seen the zoo outside my building? I respond with

"Huh?" She quickly fills me in that the local media and press are outside. I shrugged it off, not giving it a second thought.

I then relate to her what I think is appropriate with regards to my trip. I tell her about the merger and my new acquisition of Havisham Development. She is ecstatic and she has heard the news as it is all over the paper and the internet. Then she says that's why the media is outside! This didn't cross my mind, but it's probably true. Fuck! Something else I need to deal with. I tell Cassandra I am not making any statement at this time.

We then discuss all the business transactions that happened at the office over my absence, which I am up to date on anyways. Then I ask quietly, "So tell me what has been happening around the office. What rumours are floating around about my leave of absence?" She looks at me to say, really you want to gossip now!

She says, "Estella, no one questions you. But a lot of shit happened to you before you went to see your aunt. You were seeing Mr. Donaldson, and you never told me about that. And I tried several times to make you spill, but you always brought it back to business. So, before I say anything to you about the local office gossip, what happened between you two?" I knew she would bring him up! That's why I mentioned office gossip for this exact purpose.

I tell her with my controlled tone, "Nothing happened. We hung out and he wasn't for me. End of story." She looks at me, then says.

"Bullshit, you were so swooned by him! I saw a gleam and happiness in you. For the past five years I've worked for you, I've never seen a gleam or joy in you."

I resort, "Wow, thanks!" I like her and consider her my friend because she can be brutally honest with me, and she is probably one of the only people I allow to speak to me like this.

She continues, "Estella, just tell me what happened, and why you are not seeing him anymore." I'm quiet, but I do want to confide in her, so I say.

"OK, yes he was different from who I usually see, but that difference scares me, so when the opportunity of going to see Adela came up, I took it because I was concerned about Adela, and I also wanted to end it with him and wanted space. Don't look at me like that!" She is literally glaring at me.

She says, "Why would you run away? You clearly like him, Estella. You have to call him!" Absolutely *not*! I tell her in a whisper.

"Of course I cannot do that, I'm sure he has moved on. It's been a month and a bit. Plus, it was nothing, so stop freaking out. We don't even know each other. We have only seen each other for a week or so!"

She continues with, "I know what I saw in you, that week before you went away you were a different woman. You were simply happy." She is, of course, right, but it's too late. I've fucked that up.

I tell her, "Sweetie, it's over. Even if you are right, it's been too long. He probably has moved on."

"Can you just call him please?" she pleads. I realize that she is not giving up, so I succumb to her request, and tell her I will tomorrow. I can't believe I have agreed to call him, but Cassandra is absolutely right. I do like him, and I miss him. It's a weird feeling to miss or like a man. It's scary, but I want to explore these feelings further if I can. If he has moved on, it might hurt, but I'm willing to take that risk as I finally come to the realization that I'm hurting without him.

The next day that realization does not dwindle but manifests itself into me going for a lunch stroll around the law firm he works at. Yes, this might be considered stocking, but I couldn't just call him! And if he has moved on, that would hurt too much if I face him. So instead of calling or even getting my PI involve, I decide to bump into him casually and unexpectedly at a local eatery I know he frequents.

As I wait by a convenient store around his office, I see him pop out of the building. That warm, tingling feeling deep inside me stir once again. I desire him and need him at this very moment. I watch him cross the street to my side, then walk towards the sandwich shop. He lingers at the door, and suddenly this beautiful blond steps out of a cab. She hugs him warmly, and he pecks her on both cheeks, and they make their way into the shop!

What the fuck! My worst fears have materialized in front of me! Did I really need to see this? This is why I don't date or have boyfriends or fall in love! I don't need to be hurt by anyone! My own mother abandoned me by overdosing and leaving me to Ms. Havisham. This is why I cannot fall in love or trust anyone. I will not let this hurt or crush me. He means nothing to me. As per usual, Adela is spot on about men.

As I make my way back to my office, I breadth in the cool air. Summer is close, and I'm resolved to let this not get to me. I have a lot on my plate, and I plan to just submerge myself into it. James Donaldson is officially dead to me.

I step onto my floor and Cassandra has a stack of files for me. I tell her unless they are utterly important give them to Darcy. The rest she can leave on my desk. My tone and demeanour set her back, and she knows not to meddle or ask questions at this time. So, she does what she is told and leaves. I have two files I need to read and sign then a few others I need to skim. Before I could bring myself to do this, I go into my bathroom and wash my face. I look pale and sad. Then the tears just start rushing out of me. I don't normally cry, and this is the second time I cried in the last few weeks. I think before that cry, I cried was at fourteen when the girls at Loretta Abbey Private School chose not to be my friend because I was adopted.

I allow myself to sob for five minutes, then I wash my face again, and return to my desk. I will not let this get to me. I buzz Cassandra, "Can you RSVP me to Mr. Yamamoto's dinner party on Saturday. Thanks," and I hang up. I start reviewing those files.

At six, as I am packing up to leave and Cassandra comes in. I'm about to yell at her, but she looks serious, and I instinctively know this has nothing to do with James. She says, "I just got a call from Tom Calloway. He wanted to speak to you, but he said your cell was going to voice mail. I told him I will let you know." Tom! What does he want? He has moved on with his life, found some southern bell and is to be married to her. I heard or I should say know, he abuses her.

I tell her, "Thanks. I'm sorry I was so harsh earlier. I am under a lot of stress. I didn't mean to take it out on you." I mean this apology, she's a good assistant and friend.

She says, still with a concerned tone, "Its fine, but what will you do with Tom?"

I reassure her, "Nothing, I'll call him back and see what he wants. Don't worry about him, he's not a threat to me." I'm a bit surprised that Cassandra is so worried about Tom. He's not a threat. I ask her, "Why are you so worried about Tom?"

She continues, "Well, I don't like him or trust him. I think you should stare clear of him. He gives me the creeps too." This is cute and funny; I reassure her again not to worry about Tom. He really has nothing incriminating on me nor can he hurt me. I also notice that during this conversation she stares clear from the topic of James. So, I do something that is uncharacteristic, and give her hug, then say.

"Thanks for being a friend." When I pull away, I notice Pierre is already waiting at the foyer to take me home. I'll deal with Tom Calloway tomorrow.

Chapter 10

It's Friday, and I have a lot to do. I pride myself on being successful by overseeing all the important mergers and transactions that are happening in my company. Now I need to be caught up with the development company as well. Although for as long as I could remember I have been helping Adela with this company, so it's certainly not a new enterprise for me. But nevertheless, I need to clean up a bit and ensure this machine is running smoothly and productively. So, I spend most of the morning reviewing files, and large-scale developments that Havisham has undertaken in the last two years, which are eleven. I check and double check the first five and I'll do the others tomorrow. My legal team is also reviewing them.

I take a break and decide to call my ex-husband. The phone rings, "Hi Tom, it's Estella. How can I help you?" I can handle men like Tom because I know how they think, and I could never fall in love with a man like Tom.

He says, "Hi Estella, how are you?" He's playing his stupid game. I quickly say.

"I'm fine Tom, just really busy." So cut to the chase.

"As always, right? I called because I miss you and I was thinking about you. Don't start protesting, but I really miss you. I thought time would allow me to get over you, but after seeing the article of you in the papers, it just pulled at my heart." What papers? I ask him.

"What are you talking about? What papers?"

He continues, "I get the gazette from Seattle emailed to me, and it has an exposition of your takeover of Havisham Real-Estate Development Company." Why wasn't I told about this article? I quickly email one of my lawyers.

I tell him, "That should not be public knowledge yet, but yes I'm the new CEO."

He says, "Estella, congratulations, but that's not why I'm calling. Everyone knew you are going to get everything she has, so that's not surprising. I'm calling because I'm still so much in love with you. And I need you." Fuck, Tom not now.

I tell him, "Tom, don't be ridiculous, I don't love you. You are just infatuated with me or lusting for me, in any case it's not love. Plus, aren't you engaged to someone your parents can really be proud of?"

He quickly answers with, "Married, actually. But I don't care or love her. The only woman I ever loved is you. You were the centre of my universe and my life made sense when you and I were together. Now it's just a hallow shell." Ms. Havisham would be so proud of me for totally crushing this man.

I tell him, "You were married to someone who didn't love you. You were being controlled at every step. Be happy you got out of that situation, and you have a very,

very successful career and someone who can love you back." I do feel bad for the control I had over him.

He tells me, "Estella, I felt alive with you, I feel empty now. So, say what you want, but you are wrong. I want you back. You claim not to love me, then fine, that's what I desire—a loveless marriage with you."

What is he doing? I tell him, "Tom, enough. This sounds ridiculous, and no I don't want you back. Now hang up and go home to your wife. Goodbye." I hang up. I am too busy to deal with this. This ended three years ago, and I guess he remarried recently. He needs to move on. I have enough to think about, like the lack of a personal life or a suitable partner. And I'm certainly not into just fucking Tom. I'm no home wrecker, even though technically he was married to me first. No, I don't want or desire Tom. He needs to leave me alone.

After the breakup, he called and messaged me an obscene amount of times. I stopped taking his calls, and after a few months they stopped. He apparently submerged himself into his work and got a lot of attention and merits for it. Then he met his southern bell wife, and after 8 months, the two were engaged. Before he proposed to her, he called me to see what I thought. I reassured him it was the right thing to do and reaffirm there was no more of us. I guess he married her, and I thought that was the end of Tom. Hopefully, the message is clear now and he backs off.

***

I go for my usually stroll. I head into a coffee shop just to sit, have a tea and clear my head of today's events. As I flip through my emails, I look up and who do I see but Mr. Donaldson! Our eyes meet and he heads over to me. Fuck what do I say to him. Anger boils inside me as I think of him with the 'other' woman! But who am I to blame him for moving on? I didn't contact him for six weeks. However, I thought he was really into me. I thought I had him wrapped around my little fingers so to speak. I guess I'm getting rusty at this game. I need to get my head back into the game and treat him like any other douche bag.

He comes over and I greet him with a cool smile, and say, "Mr. Donaldson, how are you?"

He looks at me like I have three heads or something; he looks hurt and confused. He says, "Hi, where have you been? Why haven't you contacted me? What did I do?" Where should I begin?! I am not the one who moved on after a few weeks. So, he wants to play the victim, I can play that game too.

"I was in New Hampshire with my benefactor. I told you that," I say nonchalantly. He looks so good. Those beautiful green eyes are glistening, and he has his hair slick back. The new girlfriend probably likes it that way. As I am pondering my phone buzzes, and I say, "I really need to take this. It was great seeing you again." I then get up and simply walk away. I don't dare turn back because I know his mouth is open and he is dumbfounded that I just left so nonchalantly. I know he still likes me, regardless of the new girlfriend, but I would never give him a second chance. He ought to have waited longer for me. So yes, I hope I bring him some pain.

I feel good as I briskly walk back to my office. Then as I head to the elevator my heart sink. I miss him. Maybe abandoning him for that length of time wasn't a good idea but if he truly liked me, he would have tried harder to contact me or at least waited longer before moving on. But I can't let this get me down, I have too much going on. As I step into my office, Cassandra comes in. She instinctively knows something is not right with me.

"Are you OK? I know you don't want to talk, but I'm here if you need me," she says, expecting me to say no thanks, and change the subject to business. But not today, instead of shooing her away, I get up and close the door.

"I want to talk," I tell her. She looks shocked but sits down and says.

"Yes, please Estella. What's going on?"

"He found someone else when I was away. I do miss him, but I saw him last week with a beautiful blond. So, end of story," I tell her. Fuck it hurts to say it out loud. She thinks for a second then continues with.

"Are you sure he's with her? I mean it could be a client?"

"I saw the interaction, there was a familiarity between them that wasn't business related. I'm sure they are involved. You know what's funny, he's probably the only guy that I ever felt like this towards. It's messing with my head, and I need to get it under control," I calmly tell her. She thinks for a little then says.

"Why don't you talk to him. See where he's at?"

No! I blew him off today. I tell her, "I can't. I had a run in with him today, and I know he's still interested, but I was mad that he would move on so fast, so I moved on as well and made sure he knew it!" She doesn't seem surprised by my behaviours. Emphatically she says.

"OK, I get it. You don't usually put yourself out there. So, him moving on has really hurt you. But don't give up on finding someone. The perfect guy for you is out there."

Is she nuts? If Havisham hears her, she would have her committed to the looney house. No way am I looking for some 'special' guy, right now I feel stupid for conjuring any sort of feelings for this man. I need a new distraction quickly. Maybe the stockbroker I met a while back. He was cocky and good looking; I didn't procure him because I was bored of his type at the time. Now I need to fuck someone as a distraction from these so call stupid feelings.

I don't mention this to Cassandra of course, but I tell her, "OK, so now you know how I feel. I'll be fine. It was good getting this off my chest." I pause for a second then say, "I think I found a solution."

She asks, "*Really? What?*"

I tell her, "Don't worry your head about that. I'll be OK. So back to business," translation, this conversation is over.

Chapter 11

The following week, I contact the stockbroker and arrange a dinner. I hate doing dinners with potential partners because I find the conversations trite and dull. However, I need to get an idea if he's a good candidate for me and if there's some sort of physical attraction between us. To be honest right now the only person that I can think about is James, having sex with him, touching him, feeling his body! I clearly need to get over him.

So, I'm forcing myself to go to dinner with the stockbroker as I need to get out of this funk. I show up to the dinner, and he's all decked out with a white shirt that's not all the way buttoned, and black slacks. He looks good, but still no sort of interest is stirring inside me. He says, "Wow, you look incredible. The first time I met you, I thought she is really something." *Fuck is this going to be his lines tonight?* I don't think I'm up for this.

I tell him, "Hi, thanks. You look nice too." In an almost bored voice. I choose the restaurant of course. It's an out of the way place where no one will recognize me.

He continues in an excited tone with, "I know some great restaurants in the city, next time I'll pick the locale. Man, I had a crazy day today. I closed this big deal around eighty dollars thou! So, I'm super pumped tonight!" *Are you fucking kidding me?* He sounds like an adolescent.

I say in a bored tone, "That's interesting." And before I can say anything else, he goes into details about his big deal. I quickly message Pierre to get the car ready. After ten minutes of him raving on about his day to me, I cut him off by saying, "I'm so sorry I have to do this, but something has come up. I need to leave." Before he says anything, I get up and exit. It is rude of me, but my time is quite valuable so I'm not going to waste it here with this person.

As I sit in the back of the SUV, I ponder what my life will be like now. The old me would eat that guy up. He would be an easy target and I would probably keep him around for a bit just to make him beg for me, but I have no interest in him now. Sure, he is physically what I'm looking for, but I don't want anything to do with him physically. I think I'm resolved to be an old spinster like Adela. Fuck the plan to hurt people, the new plan is to just be by myself for a while or forever.

Back at my home, as I'm about to open a bottle of Merlot and settle into a quiet evening, my phone buzzes and Pierre tells me that Mr. Donaldson would like a word. Oh, how fitting! What an evening! "OK, send him up" I tell Pierre in a loud, sarcastic voice.

I wait by the elevator, a little pissed off from everything that has been happening with regards to my personal life. I plan on telling him off as I find that he's the author of a lot of these feelings. The door opens, and there he stands. I have missed him so much, but I try and control myself (all I want to do is to throw my arms around him). Instead, I compose myself and say, "Hello."

He responds with grabbing me and hugging me. At first, I sink into him, but then I quickly pull away and readjust my posture. "*What's that?*" I ask him.

He says, "I'm sorry, I just couldn't help myself. I have missed you so much." All I could think of is yeah, right!

I exclaim, "How's your new girl?" I figure I should just cut to the chase and end this conversation.

He looks at me perplex, then responds with, "What new girl?" Oh, so this is the game he plans on playing? I can play that game too.

"Whatever, I'm over it. How can I help you?" I ask nonchalantly.

"No, don't brush this off, seriously what girl? Since you left to go to your aunt's place, I did not hear from you. And you have been back for over a week, and you didn't contact me. What's going on? Did I do something to anger you? I thought we were enjoying each other's company. Am I the only one feeling this way?" He stops, clearly exhausted from his pleading to me. How do I respond to this? I don't want my emotions to get the best of me. Control has always been my philosophy in life.

I take a deep breath, then I say quietly, "OK, so here's the deal—too many emotions were being exchanged before I went to my benefactor. I needed a break, but during that break I realized that I really missed you, which, of course, are not emotions I'm accustomed to. So, upon my return I went to see you, only to find that you were hugging and kissing a pretty blond. I don't blame you for moving on. I mean, I left you for six weeks and did not once contact you. So, I shouldn't be upset." He's very quiet and does not respond. I move on, "Well, are you going to say something?" He's testing my patience! I can't believe I told him all that, but I needed to get it off my chest.

After an eternity it seems like he says with a smile on his face, "I was really worried about you leaving and I wanted to be there for you, but you clearly didn't want my help. I feel we share something special, and I would never move on without talking to you first. Estella, I feel a deep connection to you, which is not something I've felt before with anyone. I know we only saw each other for a short time but I really loved every second of that time. So, I am willing to invest my time and emotions into this to see where it will lead us. And I have not given up on us."

That makes me feel warm inside, but the blond! I take a slight step back, bracing myself for this and then ask, "What about the blond?" I look at him intently, fully knowing he is choosing to postpone that explanation. Then he says, "Estella, she is my sister. There is no other woman in my life." I don't know what got over me, but I sprint into his arms and bury my head in his chest. I am so elated with delight. I then kiss him passionately.

Finally, I let him breath, then say, "I'm sorry, these emotions are weird and new. But I'm so happy right now." He hugs me back and kisses me again.

He says, "I want to get to know you more, but you can't just disappear on me. I know you don't have relationships, and you have been very upfront with who you are, but I think you should relax a bit and let what happens happen. This, us, feels so right and good. Don't be afraid if it's not fitting into your definition of a relationship."—Spoken like a true lawyer.

I pull away from him, then exasperatedly say, "You don't understand me and maybe one day you will. I'm really fucked up when it comes to emotions and relationships. I was never in love, I don't really believe that even exists. I love control and see men as animals that need to be controlled. I don't do romance or feelings. My marriage was merely a loveless contract. I see the world as contracts—devoid of feelings. And this has changed since I met you. I feel excitement when you walk into a room, and it tingles inside me when you touch me. I have never felt this. I also feel vulnerable. Maybe it's menopause." I gesture with hands and then end it with a chuckle—I feel vulnerable in front of him.

He thinks for a second then with a weary smile says, "I can't begin to understand what your life has been like, and I do want to know all of it. But I'll never push you, whenever you are comfortable you can share. That being said, I don't want a non-emotional relationship—the one I agreed to initially because at this point, I care about you immensely even though it's only been a really short time." He stops, then looks at me with those beautiful, loving, sincere eyes.

OK this is a big change for me. I can't define how I feel or what's happening here. I don't know what to say to him. Typically, I would end it, as he has confessed that he wants more than a non-emotional relationship. But isn't that what I want with him? I have no idea what to do with these feeling; I am a person of habit; I like what I'm used to. I finally say, "OK, I know what you asking for but I can't make any promises. I just can't because I'm not use to these feelings. Feelings period! My life has always been voided of emotions, so this will take some time to think about and sort for me." I really want this right now, but I have no idea if this is just a passing feeling. I certainly do not want to hurt him.

I go over to him and kiss him on the cheek. Right now, I want to feel him inside me. He says, "OK we can figure this out as we go. Just talk to me about how you feel, don't run away." With that I take off his shirt and unbutton his pants.

I whisper, "I miss this, I miss you." He takes off his pants and takes off my shirt. I am not wearing a bra, so he cups my breasts and starts sucking on the right one, then the left. It feels so good. I want him to put his fingers inside me. I take his hand and hike up my pencil skirt, he kisses me hard and inserts two fingers inside me.

I see his manhood protruding through his boxers, so I take them off. I start gently stroking him, then I break away from his touch. I kneel in front of him and begin kissing his penis, slowly sucking it, then faster and harder. He's about to come and I stop. I want him inside me. He gently pushes me on the couch and then enters me and I just mould to his body. He's so big and hard inside me, I can feel every inch of him. I build and I feel him building too. I scream as I come and he orgasms shortly after. I sink on to him and we fall asleep.

Around three-thirty-three a.m. my usual hour, I wake up to find myself wrapped in his arms. I slip out off the couch, throw on a silk robe and go into my office. I sit by the huge eastern bay window. The city is alive with many twinkling lights and little to no stars, its overcast. It will probably rain tomorrow. I love the silence of the night and I would never interrupt it with work or conversation; it is just a time to ponder and reminisce about life. I used to wake up every night at this time when I was a teenager and in my early twenties. It reminds of my independence and strength. It's a time to truly be on your own.

As I reflect on last night, it hits me that maybe I'm transitioning into another aspect of life; maybe some shrink might even say growing up? I don't know, it seems complicated, and I am unsure about who I'm becoming. I welcome the time when I only view men as chattel, who I can play with, destroy and throw away. But James is different; I don't want to ever hurt him. I want him to like me and even enjoy my company. But what if this is just a fleeting feeling or worse, what if he becomes bored and tired of my weirdness, and he leaves me? That would crush me. This is why I never wanted to have any sort of feelings for another person. It gives them power over me, which obviously concerns me. No one has ever had any sort of power over me, and this man I just met has a lot of it.

As I watch the first few rays of sunshine coming into the horizon, James slips himself behind me. He's wrapped up in a blanket and naked underneath. He opens it and cocoons me; I feel his warm body on mine, and I turn around to embrace him. He unwraps himself then lifts me up and takes me to bed. I sink into his arm, and I'm transported into a sweet dream of fragrance and summer blooms.

I wake with a little shriek and realize I'm alone in bed. Was it all a blissful dream? I check the time, its ten a.m. I haven't slept in like this since I was sixteen! I spring out of bed to find myself naked. Then I hear James talking to Mrs. Anderson in the kitchen, so it wasn't a dream. I smile to myself thinking of him as I pop into my bathroom to brush my teeth and shower. As I enter the bedroom, I'm greeted by this beautiful man with a breakfast tray and fresh roses.

"Hi, wow this looks delicious. When did you have time to prepare all this? I really slept in, didn't I?" I'm rambling because I don't know what to say to all this.

He says, "You were out cold! And I can't take all the credit, Mrs. Anderson made the food, and I went out for the flowers and coffee."

I respond with, "Mmm coffee, give please." I savour the hot beverage and watch James devour his eggs, bacon and toast.

In between bites he says, "You don't eat much, do you?"

I tell him, "I do... I like my pancakes that Mrs. Anderson makes, but I'm intrigued by watching you. It's like seeing a hungry lion devour his prey!" I laugh and James does too. We eat our breakfast and chat about the day. He wants me to come with him to his friend's birthday party later this evening. I'm not one for public attention, plus I'm nervous about how he will describe me to his friends. I shudder at the term girlfriend. But I do want to see what his life is like, who his friends are etc. "OK, I'll come," I tell him with a smile on my face. He launches towards me and kisses me on the lips. Mmmm he tastes yummy. I neglect to tell him I'll have to give away my Givenchy fashion show tickets for today. I'll send my personal stylist to the event instead.

It's Saturday, and the day is filled with a leisurely walk in Central Park and a stop for ice cream. We sit together on a bench, and I rest my head on his arm. He feels heavenly. "Do you like living in the city?" I suddenly ask him.

He responds with "Yes, for now as I build my name and clients. But I don't think I can live here forever. How about you? Would you ever move?" I never thought about this, I mean if I want to grow old in the city.

I say, "I have never really thought about moving. I don't know how I feel about growing old here. I mean my company is based here so it makes sense for me to stay here. And I have businesses all over the world including a huge company in Seattle, but I think New York city is a better base for that one. Although this city can be overwhelming at times, and I do like the quiet too."

He consents saying, "Yes, it can! Would you ever move later on in life?"

I think for a second, then say, "Yes, I'm not opposed to moving to somewhere quieter."

Then I excitedly tell him, "Oh, I forgot to tell you, but you are looking at the new and sole proprietor of Havisham Development Cooperation!" Of course, my professional life is none of his business, but I feel the need to share everything with this man.

He says, "Is that your aunt's company? I saw something in the papers. Is that a good thing? Wouldn't you have a lot on your plate?"

Of course, he already knew I inherited the company but that was not the reaction I expected, but I say, "I'm quite capable of managing that company. I have been involved with it all my life. So, I'm not worried; I need to make a few senior management positions and move that headquarter to New York, but the company really runs itself." I think that should suffice his curiosity!

He continues with, "OK, OK. I'll back off. I know you are very capable Ms. Havisham. I was just worried about your wellbeing. But thinking of it now—OK, I know you can handle it. My dear, you are an extraordinary woman." Ha, nice back peddling.

I look at him with a sly grin, then say, "Thanks, I think." He knows I'm not very happy with his comment, it's weird how he can read my mind.

"Listen, I'm not trying to stick my nose in your business, but I'm worried about you and this seems like a lot for anybody. I just want to make sure you are physically and mentally well."

I sigh, then say, "Of course I will be fine. Don't worry about me. How about you? What's going on at your firm?"

He knows I am changing subjects, so he says, "It's going good. I am thinking of opening my own firm with the clients I have. That's my short-term goal."

I tell him, "That's exciting. Is there anything I can do to help?" My connection and name alone can give him a very lucrative client list. I have never thought to offer him help before.

He says with a laugh, "Thanks, your name alone would ensure all the big wig companies, but I would never feel right about you helping my career. So, thank you for the kind offer, but I want to do this on my own merits."

I can respect that, but I say, "Are you sure? One phone call from me will ensure you have some impressive clienteles, including myself." I stop there, I have thought about him heading up my legal team but I'm not sure about mixing business with pleasure.

He breaks the silence by saying, "I won't be comfortable representing you. No offense, but I don't think I could do a good job representing you and personally being involved with you. If it's OK with you, I would like to keep the two separate and just work on my own merits." He finishes with an adorable smile and a wink. I like him a little more after that revelation.

I then hug him and say, "OK."

We head back to Pierre, and I drop James to his place. He will pick me up in an hour or so. This is new as no one picks me up since Tom! I go home and take a long shower. After I call up Cassandra to give away my front row fashion seats to my stylist. Then I go into my oversize closet with a glass of merlot and sit at my dresser. I think about James and his refusal to take my help. I think I might have insulted him or maybe even emasculated him by my suggestion. But he's got to understand I have a very dominant personality, and normally, actually always, get what I want. Love is not something I ever wanted though. There's so much to think about and I don't want to do it tonight. I choose a skimpy Givenchy black dress that extenuates all my best assets. I look hot if I must say, and I pair the dress well with tan Louboutin pumps and a Birkin bag. Yes, this will do. My buzzer rings, it's Pierre. I tell him to bring Mr. Donaldson up.

Chapter 12

As the door opens, both Pierre and James' mouths drop open. I say, "Boys, pick up your tongues off my rug!" They are both in awe of me, and although I like the attention, I become shy. So, I say, "James, do you want a drink?" He composes himself and accepts the offer. I drink the Merlot I opened earlier, while James sips on a beer. He looks amazingly cool and hot. He's sporting a Polo Ralf Lauren golf shirt and jeans. I look a little overdress compared to him, but I'm always overdressed. I prefer it that way. I'm not a casual person when I go out.

I ask him, "Are you nervous about me meeting your friends?"

This takes him by surprise, he says, "No, not in the least. You will blow their breaths away! Are you nervous?" Are you kidding me? I make multimillion dollar deals every day, meeting his friends does not make me nervous!

I tell him, "Of course not. But this is a first for me; I don't do the friend thing."

He smiles and says, "Thanks for making the exception." I squeeze his hand, then we head down to his car.

The restaurant is trendy, I have been here twice for business dinners. The reservation is under James' friend name, so I am anonymous tonight. It's a Saturday evening and it's a bustling spot. There are lots of people at the main restaurant, but we are taken to a private room. It's a beautiful room, with lots of character. The private party is small, maybe 100 people or so. James holds my hand as we enter, I'm not comfortable with that, but I don't pull away. He says hi to someone but doesn't stop for introductions. We go to the bar, and he says, "What would you like?"

I just want water, I tell him "Sparkling water, please." He gives me a side glance but says nothing. After getting our drinks, we make our way to the birthday boy.

Fred Pinto, he's James's age, and he seems to have let himself go a little. His face is plump and red, and his gut is protruding through his shirt. I shake hands with him as James says, "Fred, I like you to meet my girlfriend, Estella." And that's the dreaded word that I'm afraid of.

I paint on a fake smile, and awkwardly say, "Great party, thanks for having me." Fred and James converse about how long it's been since they have seen each other. All this time, James is holding my hand. I squeeze his and he leads me to a somewhat private area.

He asks, "Are you OK? Is there too many people?"

He seems genuinely concerned about me, so I say, "I'm fine, just a new situation that I'm adjusting to."

With that we head to more people where James introduces me, and one woman asks, "Are you Estella

Havisham from the real estate development company? I see you all the time on Page six!" Fuck, I didn't really plan on being recognized.

OK, I can handle this, "Yes, I am. Please to meet all of you." James grips on me tightens.

I smile at him, and someone comes up and whispers something in his ear. He looks over at me and says, "Apparently, you are the local celebrity here. People recognize you!"

I look at him and say, "I'm sorry, I can leave?" I kinda do want to leave, but to be honest everyone so far has been quite nice. Fred's wife, Debra, comes up to us.

She says, "Honestly, James, you need to let go of her. We don't bite. She is ravishing!" With that she grabs my hand and takes me to another corner of the room. I notice James' apologetic look on his face, and I flash him a big smile. This is silly, I don't need a babysitter here. I'm a big girl.

Hor'douveres are being passed around, and I'm taken to a group of young professionals. Debra introduces me as, "This young lady is James' girlfriend." And everyone is quite polite and welcoming during their introductions.

One woman asks, "Is that a Birkin?" I'm not sure if I should respond to such a question, but I smile with a nod.

Someone whispers in her ear, "She is Estella Havisham!" I think this is a bit gauche, but I ignore the comment and chat with Debra. She is an Executive at Flint Thompson Wealth Management firm. I know the CEO a little too well if you know what I mean—I spanked him a few times with a black flogger and gaged him with a leather strap once.

"By the way, whatever you are doing, keep on doing it. James is so happy! We have never seen him this relaxed and just happy!" Debra says to me. This is news to me; I didn't really think of his past or his baggage.

I tell her, "Thank you. That also works both ways. He has made me a very happy woman." We chat some more, then James comes and whisks me to our table.

He asks, "Are you OK? I saw you smiling, that's why I didn't come earlier." I knew he was watching me this whole time. I could feel his eyes on me.

"I'm good, just chatting with a few of your friends," I tell him.

"I hope they told you nice things about me. Are you sure you are fine?" he asks again.

I respond, "Yeah, I'm good. Don't worry about me. Your friends are nice." I don't mention my irritation to the Birkin comment or the fact they are all whispering about who I am. We can discuss that later.

I feel all eyes are on us. So, I tell James, "I think people are either really fascinated by us or see me as a circus freak."

He sighs and says, "Unfortunately, everyone figured out you are some wealthy woman who graces the newspaper all the time. I'm sorry about the attention. If you want, we can leave. I didn't think everyone would recognize you." I know he didn't intend for this to happen.

I say, "Don't worry about it. I'm used to attention. I don't care what these people think of me."

We sit at a table with some of James' friends. They are either current work colleagues or high school friends. All of them, including their wives or partners, are very welcoming and kind. I like his friends. I like this feeling of being his girlfriend. It doesn't feel awkward, but nice and natural when I'm beside him. When Tom was courting me, we didn't do the friends thing. We did the who's who of high society, but these people were not our friends.

After dinner we pass the night by chatting with various people. Some of them personally know my employees and we chat a bit about business and other topics. Then James pulls me onto the dance floor. My mood is jovial, so I indulge him by dancing to an old pop song. We laugh at the choice and then head outside for a breather. He's happy with the night so far. He says, "Are you sure you are OK? And how come you are not drinking?"

I don't like drinking too much in public, so I tell him, "I had two glasses of wine at home, and that's my limit for the evening. But I am having so much fun! Thank you for inviting me!" He pulls me closer and kisses me hard and deep.

"Can we go home now?" he asks. He reads my mind.

"Yes, please!" I respond. We say our goodbyes to everyone, and James spends a little time congratulating the birthday boy again. I am happy I conceded to come.

On the car ride home, James and I chat about his friends, then he asks, "OK this might be too soon, but I would love it if you came with me to Washington where I grew up. My dad is having his sixtieth in a month, and my family is throwing him a party. Can you join me for a couple of days? No pressure, just think about it and if it's too much, too soon for you I will understand." Wow, that's a lot—to meet his parents and all his family is a lot. I hated Tom's family, even though I grew up knowing them.

"I'll think about it, but I'm not the meet the family type of gal." I tell him.

He says, "I know, and thanks for thinking about it."

After five minutes of not thinking about this I say, "OK, then you have to come with me next Saturday to a work event in Paris. We will go Saturday in the morning and should be back on Wednesday night. It's a work/charity event that my telecommunication company is involved in—it's a campaign to help foster kids around the world. It's also a good way for me to network in Europe and help a charity that is close to my heart." I almost forgot about this event; it's a pain to travel at this busy time, but I do want to advertise more in the European market and help a good charity. I add, "Cassandra, my assistant, will contact you with all the details."

He finally says, "That's quite the trip, but sure I'm in! Do I need to book a flight?"

I smirk at him and say, "No, one of my jets will take us. Cassandra will arrange everything."

He couldn't help saying, "One of your jets? How many do you have?"

I laugh, then say nonchalantly, "Only two, one for my old company and the newly acquired one from Havisham Inc."

He smiles, then says with a lot of glee in his tone, "So, does this mean you are coming with me to Washington?"

With a weary smile I say, "Yes." I then hug and kiss him.

When we get to his place, he invites me up for a night cap. I quickly message Pierre to be ready to pick me up, but I know James will want me to spend the night. We enter his apartment, and I ask him to pour me a glass of brandy. As I sip the warm liquid, I inquire, "Do you have any restraints?"

He looks at me with a wicked smile and says, "I'm sure I can find some." He goes to his closet and hunts around, then comes up with two pieces of ropes, which will do. I quickly take them from him and gulp down my drink. Then I lead him into his bedroom.

I gently push him on to the bed and remove his pants. Then I undo his shirt and expose that beautiful chest of his. I kiss his chest then his belly, and I see his penis growing right below my lips. I restrain his right hand onto the bed post then the left and I remove his boxers. He says, "Are you being naughty tonight, Ms. Havisham?"

I respond with, "I plan on being very naughty tonight, Mr. Donaldson. Tell me if it's too much, please."

He says, "I'm sure I can take it, but I will." Although I don't want to hurt him, sometimes I get carried away. I start by biting and tugging on his nipples, he squirms in pleasure and pain. I then give him little bites on his chest. He continues to squirm; I go between his legs and bite his inner thigh. Then move onto gently kissing his penis. I start sucking harder, and he moans my name. I bite down gently, then a little harder he looks at me and I smile. I move up and kiss him passionately. Then I climb on top of him. I let the tip of his penis slide inside me. I'm so wet, so I put all his penis inside. He wants to control the rhythm, but he can't. He moans loudly and just surrenders his body to me. I control the speed of him entering me, then when he's about to come I get off. I quickly undo his restraints and tell him to fuck me hard. And fuck he does, so hard with so much force and passion. I scream his name as I orgasm and he screams mine as he comes shortly after.

I sink into his arms and drift into a deep sleep. I dream about strange animals chasing James and I. He is trying to safeguard me against the animals. I wake up with a start to find myself entangle with James. He looks so peaceful as he sleeps, there is even a slight smile on his face. I shudder as I think this is feeling too comfortable. I'm starting to depend on this man, and my feelings for him is developing fast and furious. This scares me, so I quietly and gently slip out of his arms and legs and get myself dress. It's five am, I message Pierre and go outside to wait for him. It's a beautiful late spring Sunday morning. As Pierre pulls up, I get in and tell him to take me home.

An idea has popped into my head. I want to go to church. I have not been since I was twelve, but I have an urge to do so at this very moment. I quickly shower and get dress, then check my emails and messages from yesterday—not much and nothing of importance. I feel the need to find an answer to my dilemma, so I am turning to God. I am not particularly religious, obviously, but I do believe in God. I was not raised in a religious household, but on occasions Berta would take me to a few Catholic masses. Religion was never foremost in my upbringing. Plus, my life has been anything but ideal, so I did not embrace God or the church much in the past. But this whatever it is with James, feels unlike anything I have experienced, and I don't want to screw it up or be hurt by it either.

I slip into the last bench at a little Catholic parish Pierre has driven me to. The sermon has just started, so I listen carefully. The message is giving back when you have abundance and remembering those in need. After the sermon, I listen to the homily and in my mind, I begin to pray to God. I ask for forgiveness, and guidance. I end my silent prayer with thanks to what I currently have amass. I make the sign of the cross. It's a packed church, but I don't really pay much attention to the congregation. After the mass I go up to the alter and kiss the Virgin Mary's feet, I then leave.

I ask Pierre to drive me to little restaurant for a lunch meeting with Cassandra. As I reflect on last night and this morning, I feel light and at peace. I look down at my phone and noticed a miss call and three messages from James. I read the messages and listen to his voice mail. He misses me and wants to spend Sunday morning feeding me pancakes. This puts a smile on my face. I write back that I need to work but will meet him for coffee after my meeting. I smile as I conclude my message with a kiss emoji. This feels right; he feels right. I know I am getting a second chance at this thing we call life.

The meeting with Cassandra is quite productive. We plan my week, and she knows the particulars of Paris. As she leaves, I call up Ms. Havisham. I have been ignoring her calls for a week, so I figure this was the best time. After a ring I say, "Hi Adela, it's me. How have you been?"

Her voice is faint, she says, "Estella, why haven't you answer my calls? You need to be more responsive to me!" Here we go, she continues, "How have you been?"

I say, "Very busy being the CEO of two big companies. How are you feeling?" I don't want to lie to her, so I avoid talking about myself.

She says in a brisker tone, "I'm fine, I noticed you fired Grimbsley, he was a good VP, and an old friend. But I trust your judgment." I knew this call was coming; he's old money and a relic, so I needed to get rid of him and focus on the modern market. Say what you will about Adela, she is smart and understands money.

"Thanks aunt, I appreciate your trust in me," I tell her because I know she doesn't do well with compliments, and the fact that I called her aunt is reeling in her head.

She continues, "Another reason I wanted to speak to you is Helen, you know Arthur's daughter, she wants to meet with you in New York." This is news, these people always treated me as an outsider. They frankly despise me because they think I am not truly a Havisham and they know I am Adela's sole heiress.

I ask, "Why?"

She quickly responds with, "I guess they heard about you taking over the company. Arthur has been calling me nonstop, I refused his calls. I cannot deal with them, Estella."

I ask her, "How do you know Helen wants to see me?"

She responds with, "She left a message with Berta. I want to give you the heads up because they might end up stalking you. I'm a recluse so no chance of that for me." I shudder at the thought of meeting with this woman. I ask Havisham "What do you want me to do?"

She says, "I don't care. You are a grown woman, tell them the truth or not. Shun her or see her, just don't invite her to your house. I want to see you soon. When will you come over?" I tell her I'm busy right now, maybe in a few weeks. We talk a bit more about the company, then we conclude the conversation.

This is a lot to think about. I really hate Helen and her pretentious brother. They were so mean to me whenever I saw them. Adela could not tolerate them partly because she dislikes her brother. Arthur had three children, my mother—Christina, Helen and Thomas. Helen and Thomas were much older than me, but I saw how spoiled, over indulged, and quite rude they were when I was a child. Of course, they had no idea I was their niece.

I check the time, and message James to meet me at the restaurant. It's already three p.m. and if I leave the restaurant I'll just want to go home and sleep. Twenty minutes later he's pulling up in his Benz on the opposite street besides the restaurant. Then as he walks into the establishment all eyes follow his trail. He's steaming hot!

"Hi, how did you sleep?" I greet him. He bends over and plants a kiss on my forehead.

He tells me casually, "Good but I woke up alone. I was not overjoyed by that."

I tell him, "Sorry, I had a lot on my mind. I went to church this morning. Then had a lunch meeting with my assistant and a lengthy conversation with my benefactor. Plus, I was very productive today!"

He looks at me with an odd look and says, "Church?"

I smile and say, "It's been a while, but I'm a believer."

He continues, "did I bring this on?"

I respond, "Yes, kind of. I needed some guidance because this is a new territory for me. I feel at peace now, so don't worry your pretty little head." This should suffice him for now.

He continues with, "What did Ms. Havisham want?" I feel a deep-rooted need to be honest with him, so I tell him about Helen and Arthur wanting a meeting with me.

Then I tell him, "These people were very nasty to me. They always made me feel like an outsider."

With warmth in his eyes he says, "I am sorry to hear that. No child deserves that."

I reassure him, "Adela protected me. She was not fond of any of them, so although I was made to feel like an outsider, they all knew I was going to be the sole heiress of the Havisham's wealth. That's probably why they all hate me."

He says, "Yes, that's likely. Do you really want the Havisham legacy?"

That's an odd question, "Of course, I do. It's my name too." He doesn't know I am a Havisham.

He says, "I know it's a ton of power, money and prestige. But you can always dismantle the company and sell it off."

What a crazy suggestion, I look at him with a little disdain then say, "I don't need money. I think I'm a pretty successful businesswoman without that company. However, the Havisham estate and cooperation are more than just money. It's a family history and legacy that Adela has groomed me for since she adopted me. There is something else, I am a Havisham."

I pause and he says, "Yes, I know the name has roots and a legacy in this country, but so what? As you said they treated you like an outsider."

I tell him, "But I am a Havisham. Not a lot of people know this, and I only found out a few years ago, my mother was Arthur's oldest daughter. She, at sixteen, ran away from home, came to New York and fell into the wrong crowd I guess. Apparently, she abused drugs, then got pregnant. By that time her parents and family disowned her, and no one knew of the pregnancy, except Adela. She died during childbirth, and I was put up for adoption. A few months later Adela tracked me down and adopted me. No one knew any of this, including myself. People thought I was Adela's housemaid baby, but that was quickly rejected because she and her child moved to Vermont. I think Adela was worried that Arthur might claim me as his granddaughter, so she kept my identity quiet. I found out about three years ago when I hired a PI to investigate my birth mother. I, of course, blamed Adela and didn't speak to her for three years. During my lengthy trip to New Hampshire last month, we worked it out. It's not perfect, but I've somewhat forgiven her. She then decided after to speed up a portion of my inheritance and give me a 100 percent of the company."

He's quiet. I think he is taking everything in and processing it. He finally says, "I don't think she should have lied about who you really are. This is a lot for you or anyone to handle. Why did she give you the company now?"

I respond, "Who knows, she is quite eccentric. But I think it's her way of keeping me close to her and not losing me again."

He says, "This is a lot of pressure for you. I appreciate the legacy and the name, but still, you don't have to own this company or take on this responsibility if it's too much." Clearly this is not what I want to hear, but before getting offended I think through what he is saying.

After a few minutes I say, "I know you are thinking of my welfare, but I have thought this through and I can manage it. Plus, it's something I really want."

He smiles, then says, "OK then, I will support you in this however I can."

I feel the need to come clean. I want James to know everything about my relationship with Adela... I mean everything. I begin, "OK there is also more, I mean a lot more about my childhood you should know."

James responds with "OK, I'm listening." I begin to tell him everything, including the cold childhood, the wet nurse I had, her poisoning me on men and the brothels when I was a teenager. I tell him about the chateau in the South of France and her hatred for mankind.

James looks tired and sad. He finally says, "She abused you, Estella. I know she was your mother figure, but what you have told me is simply child abuse. I see how you feel about her but taking you to brothels as a teenager and polluting your mind about everything is wrong."

I need to defend her, but I am drained, so I say, "I know, but I'm trying to deal with that. Please let me handle it."

He continues with, "And she lied about who you really are for such a long time! Which is also unfair to Arthur because she took away his relationship with his granddaughter. And your marriage!"

I look at him with a weary look and say, "I know all of this. I don't forgive easily, but she is the only family I have. So let me deal with this my way, please."

He says, "I'm sorry, I don't mean to add more stress on you. I just think it's unjust what has happened to you." Then he unexpectedly comes over and hugs me. The conversation ends there, and we head out of the restaurant hand in hand. He walks me to Pierre, and says, "You don't need to meet them. And if you choose to, I can come with you." He then kisses me.

I tell him, "Thank you for listening and supporting me." I hug him, then say, "can we go home?" He puts me into the escalade, then follows me in his car.

At my home we take a bath together, and Mrs. Anderson prepares us some dinner. My appetite has vanished, as I move my food around the plate. James looks at me keenly but does not say anything. All I want to do is to sink into this man's arm in bed.

Chapter 13

Early Monday morning, James leaves for home to get ready for work. I urge him to bring some clothes over later. Yes, I know… a big step as I'm practically asking this man to move in! But when I say this, it doesn't even faze me… it feels natural and good. I guess I'm evolving.

Although on my car ride to the office, I'm a little shock by my 180-degree behaviour with regards to James. Am I becoming domesticated? Am I now a 'normal' girl smitten by a man? What is happening to me? I feel at peace when I'm with him, but is this truly me? The cold-hearted bitch that Havisham created to exact her revenge on men? No, I don't deserve any of this happiness; I have hurt men just to please my benefactor. I have hurt innocent people like Philip because of Adela. I don't deserve this sort of happiness. But I do understand I don't need to hurt others to feel happy, at least I don't think I do. I tell myself to stop overthinking this, just go with the flow and do what makes me happy. If that means he might hurt me, so be it. I have literally never felt this way for a man before.

My day is busy, as I'm trying to hire a new VP for Havisham Development. A lot of potential candidates are interested; however, I think I know who I want but it will take some convincing to get him on board. Cassandra has done up my schedule for Paris, and I have a brief meeting with her and Mr. Darcy.

Around two p.m. I message James, "I'm thinking of you. I miss you."

Instantly he responds with, "Me too. You are constantly on my mind. Let's have dinner tonight."

I respond with, "Would love that." As I smile into the phone, Cassandra comes in and breaks my trance.

"I need you to schedule in a trip to Washington DC for next month. I will be away for five days. Prepare as much paperwork I can take with me and arrange the jet, please." Cassandra eyes me with a wicked look because she knows I have no business there.

She asks, "Washington?"

I smile at her and say, "Yes, I'm going to meet his family for his dad's sixtieth." I can't help but beam, I continue, "I know what you are thinking, but he's so different from anyone I've ever met. He's kind and gentle. Cassandra, he makes me want to be a nicer person!" I stop, I have never divulged such personal thoughts to her.

She readily says, "Oh my god, Estella. This is great news! You deserve to feel this way! Please embrace it, he's right for you. I'm so happy for you. Don't worry about anything, I have everything under control. This is great news!"

After a second her happy expression darkens and she asks, "What about the girl?" The girl?

Oh, I tell her, "It was his sister. Can you arrange a meeting with Mr. Schmidt tomorrow at nine a.m. please."

We discuss other business, and she leaves with a big smile on her face.

After work I meet up with James at a little cafe in between our offices. I order a scone and some jasmine tea to go, and we go for a little walk on the busy streets of Manhattan. It's a warm day. We talk about our trip to Paris and I tell him I want to extend our trip to two weeks because I want to show him my summer home in Nice. He hesitantly says, "Really? I don't know if I want to see the home you suffered abuse."

I smile and say, "The chateau has great memories for me and I want to share it with. The brothels were separate." He looks a little perplex, so I change the topic by telling him I want him to accompany me to a fashion show I'm dying to see. It's the fall collection of Gucci. He chuckles but agrees.

He then says, "I didn't see you much of a fashionista. It seems below such a strong, powerful woman. Although, you do dress chic!"

I laugh at him, "I love fashion, always did. When I was a teenager I always caught the top designers spread in Europe. My personal stylist praises my choices. Hence, I like going to these shows—you'll see me in my element in Paris."

He looks at me with bewilderment, then says, "You have a personal stylist? I mean I don't know much about fashion, but that seems extreme." I can certainly tell he doesn't know much about fashion, as he's wearing a Calvin Klein suit from last year.

I don't say anything about that, but I say, "It's not extreme, I can teach you. Canali and Versace make amazing suits for men."

He cocks his head and looks at me, "No way, you are not dressing me. I'm a simple man with simple tastes."

I protest, "I am so verse in fashion, just let me do your clothing for Paris and you can have the final say on everything, please!"

He looks at me with a surrendered look, and says, "I love seeing you happy and excited, so OK. But nothing crazy, I'm not into trends or styles. I wear whatever I can find. And yes, I would love to see your summer home in Nice."

I beam at him with a big smile and say, "We can go shopping tomorrow after work!" And I quietly add for him agreeing to accompany me to Nice, "Thank you."

He says with a happy tone, "OK, but I'm paying for of this!" No, I'll treat him, but that will be tomorrow's surprise.

We go for dinner near my place, I want oysters because I feel quite naughty. At dinner I say, "Can we go to your place and get some stuff for you?"

He looks at me intrigue, and says, "Only if you eat more than oysters. The seafood pasta is fantastic here and if you eat that we can go." I pout, but I'm hungry so I oblige him. The pasta is fantastic, but I couldn't finish it. We head out to his place. In the car my phone buzzes a weird number twice. I don't pick up because I don't recognize the number. I tell myself I'll check my voice mail later. At James' place I help him pack a few toiletries and clothing. Then we head out, and my phone buzzes again. I check only to see the same number!

I excuse myself and pick up the call. I say quickly, "Hi, who's this?"

The very familiar voice says, "Estella, it's me. I have been trying to get a hold of you. I know I have a new number, sorry, but we need to meet up, maybe for a congratulatory dinner." Fuck, why now?

I say, "Thanks, I'm a bit tied up now. Can I call you tomorrow?"

Tom responds with, "That's a hallow gesture and we both know it. Is he there?" Great! He knows about James.

I say, "Good night." And hang up. This is not good; Tom is very determined and clearly not thinking straight.

I get into the car to join James. He asks, "Who was that?"

I don't lie, so I tell him, "That was my ex-husband congratulating me on my inheritance again and also to mention your existence."

He looks at me blankly and says, "He still wants you?"

I tell him, "It was a bad break up, he didn't want it. But I thought he has moved on because he found someone about a year and a half ago. They are married. I think when he found out that I was seeing you, there was a renewed interest." I stop, this must be too much for him.

He looks at me, "Why did you guys break up?"

I hate this question because he knows why I married Tom, so I say, "The marriage was a mistake you know that. I never loved him, and I got bored of him." This answer leaves some blanks to fill in.

He says, "OK, I know and we can talk about this later, but not today. I just want you in my arms and sleep." Thank *God*! This man is so good at respecting my feelings!

We head back to my place, shower together and we both just go to bed. I have become quite domesticated with my life now. In bed James has already fallen asleep and I'm quite tired too. But before I give in to sleep, I think how changed my life has become—I mean there are no collars or whips tonight, no handcuffs or even sex, just a nice dinner and then bed. The weirdest thing is, I'm quite content with the evening and night. I contemplate how tranquil my life is right now, and for the first time in years I am truly happy.

I wake up at three-twenty a.m. with a start. I cannot remember what I was dreaming about. I untangle myself from James and go down to the living room's bay window to look at the quiet city. I love staring into the dark night. Soon, I know my dear aunt will importune me with her presence. My mind starts racing, is it this relationship that is making me restless? Or Tom's persistent contact? I feel an uneasiness, and even a fear that my happiness might be short lived. I need to ensure my past doesn't ruin my future.

I think about my two companies. They are both like my children; I want to see them both strive and develop.

But is it too much for one person? Should I sell one of them and pour my heart into just one? Too many things to think about. I have the companies sedate for now. What I'm really worried about is James! Is he going to crush my bubble and leave me? What sort of damage will he do to me? Should I just end it now, and save myself from further heartbreak? Absolutely not, he's the only person that calms me down and brings me happiness. I will not just cut that out of my life. But why doesn't he press me about my relationship about Tom? Fuck, I sound like an annoying stereotypical chick!

OK, I know what I need to do! I need to deal with Tom and the Havisham clan. I am going to announce to these people I really am a Havisham and I'll also get to the bottom of Tom's issue; he needs to back off too. I like my life right now and will not have any of any of these people ruining it. I am resolved, so I slip back into bed, and hold my man tight.

Before the alarm sounds, I disengage it and head towards the shower. I then put on a pencil skirt and a Chanel blouse that makes me look like the CEO of two mega companies. I tell myself in a whispered voice – "I'm going to conquer all my problems today."

James peers at me from the covers, and says, "You are early! And you look fantastic! A big meeting today?"

I look at him and say, "Something like that. Why didn't you want to hear about my ex-marriage yesterday?"

He looks at me out of sorts and says, "I don't care about your past relationship. I'm focus on us now and the future."

I respond, "Did it bother you that he has been contacting me?"

He thinks for a second and says, "To be honest, yes because he's clearly still in love with you. Who can blame him? However, I am confident you don't feel the same for him." That's for sure!

I tell him, "Our marriage was fucked up. I had no feelings for him. He was a good match for me on paper and he obeyed me. I got bored of that after four years and left him. Unfortunately, I think he misses the dominance and is confusing that for love. Hence his repetitive need to contact me."

James asks, "What does he exactly want?"

I respond, "I'm not sure. To talk, maybe even a second chance?"

I hold my breath and wait for his response, he says, "And how do you feel about that?" He is stoned face; I cannot read him.

I say with as much honesty I can muster in my voice, "Of course, I don't want that! I never cared or loved him and whatever we had physically is long over. I want him permanently out of my life."

James smiles and says, "I knew that, that's why I didn't pursue it last night." And he then kisses me on my forehead. He adds, "You are going to be late for work!" I am relieved because I seriously thought maybe he let the

Tom thing go because he doesn't care about me. Clearly, he just sincerely believes me—again this is all new territory for me.

I tell him as I grab my blazer, "Yes I will, have a good day. I'll see you tonight." Hurriedly I plant a kiss on his lips then head to the front door. I'm running late.

At the office Cassandra has a stack of documents I need to go over, and I need to close the Japanese deal. I read over the documents, which are all in perfect order, but I hold off signing as I'm meeting with Mr. Yamamoto on Thursday for dinner. I then decide to take a stroll and call up Helen, Arthur's daughter.

She answers on the second ring and I say, "Hi, Helen its Estella. How are you?"

"Estella, I'm OK. I need to see you. When can I come by?" She asks politely. No, I don't want you to come by!

"Helen, I'm a bit busy with work stuff, can I help you with something now. What's this about?" I ask in a matching tone.

She unceremoniously says, "This would be best to do in person. It's about Havisham incorporated. My dad and I would like to meet with you." Of course, it is!

"I'm away this weekend and most of next week, but call my assistant at the office and have her schedule you in. Bye," I tell her, ending the call. Fuck them, I don't need to explain why Adela gave me her company, they can take it up with her. I wanted to tell her that I'm also a Havisham, but on second thought I certainly do not need to explain myself to anyone!

This conversation has placed a sour taste in my mouth as I head into my office, only to be greeted by Cassandra, Helen and Arthur! So, it really is going to go down now. "I'm so sorry, Ms. Havisham, but I told them that you were quite busy and could not possibly see them today!" Cassandra says apologetically.

I smile at Cassandra, and say, "See them into the conference room. I'll be there shortly." I head to my office bathroom to collect myself. I look at the mirror and tell myself, "I can do this!" I then walk into the conference room.

Arthur is comfortably sitting in my chair staring at me, while Helen is pacing in front of the window. "Hi, family, how can I help you?" I say as cheeky as possible.

Arthur starts by saying, "You certainly look well! I bet if I got a fake family's name and fortune, I would look well too. But atlas that was not meant for me!"

As he speaks my smile just gets bigger, and I interrupt him with, "But you did get, what was it two mil cash from your father's will. I would be quite happy with that."

It's true the Mr. Havisham took him off his company and estate because of his philandering when he was young, but he still left him with a sizable cash inheritance. He continues, "That's really nothing, is it now, Estella? I am a Havisham. Who exactly are you and why are you the sole owner of my father's company and estate!" He's clearly upset, and I can have security remove him in seconds, but this needs to be resolved.

I tell him calmly, "Take it up with your half-sister."

Helen, who is just standing there all this time, finally says, "She is unreachable. She is a cuckoo old lady! You need to return what is clearly not yours."

Now I'm just angry, I say, "Adela is quite capable mentally. You should have a chat one day with her, she is quite keen. As for the estate and company, I'm Adela's sole heiress, and I will not be relinquishing any of it! As for the legacy of the name. I have your name in more ways than you think." I turn and directly look at Arthur in the face, then say, "Hello, grandfather! I'm Christina's daughter if you care to know."

He looks at me with a smirk and says, "Christina did not have any kids!" All I could think of is—really? You know this because you cared about her life and took care of her during her addiction.

"You should look into that," I say instead in a matter-of-fact tone.

I go on to tell them, "I'm very busy, and to answer your petition about this inheritance—I will not be relinquishing it. You will have more luck with Adela. Now goodbye." As I say this, I buzz Cassandra and say sarcastically, "My lovely family is leaving." She knows that means get security!

As Arthur is exiting, I hear him say to Helen, "It's impossible. She did not have a baby. I would have known!" I am sure he will launch his own investigation into this, and I don't care; I am done with them.

After a few minutes of them leaving, I sit back and look out the window. What have I done? I just told a man

I was his granddaughter and still I felt no feelings and love for him, not even a little. I feel nothing towards those people. I am sorry because I know they will harass Adela now. Arthur will be venomous towards her because she adopted his granddaughter and raised her to be me—a person he has detested for so many years. I guess I should be mad at Adela for always painting a bad picture of Arthur and not giving me a chance to get to know him as a grandfather, I mean he couldn't be that bad. He is nice to Thomas and Helen. And what about Thomas and Helen? They could have been my loving uncle and aunt if they knew I was indeed a Havisham. No, the adoption should not have mattered, Arthur and them should have been nicer to a helpless little child, regardless of who I really was. These people are heartless and mean. However, I can't help but think Adela is partially responsible. I pause and try to clear mind. I'll confide in James about this later, that will help.

That evening James and I are sitting down for dinner at my place. Felix has really outdone himself. He has made chicken schnitzel with a sauerkraut salad and beet soup. We discuss our upcoming trip to France and I tell him I want to spend two weeks instead of ten days. I don't want James to be jet lag and I really want to spend a few nights at the Havisham chateau in Nice. He agrees that we should not rush France. He says to me, "Two trips back-to-back, and each with their own adventure! Are you nervous about meeting my family? You don't have to if you don't want to." He pauses, and before I can say something he continues with, "But I'm really looking forward to you meeting them!" He's so excited, and happy, I can't possibly tell him that I don't want to meet them, can I?

As we continue to chat about this Washington trip, I come around to the idea of meeting his family. I tell it would be great seeing his roots and I mean it. I want to know more about him and clearly I want him to know more about me.

I then quickly change the subject because I realized that I haven't asked him about his career initiatives. The last he told me was that he was planning on venturing out on his own. I ask, "Tell me about your work? What's happening on that front?"

He says, "Well I have my client list, so that's the hardest part. Now, I'm waiting for my lease to be signed. I found a great spot close to both of our places. So now I'm just waiting for the landlord to sign the lease."

Interesting, I ask him "What's the address?"

He says, "It's between ninth and tenth street. I think it's in the tenth street office tower building."

Very nonchalantly, I say, "That lease will be signed soon. And the new amendment will be a rent of zero dollars." I then give him a little smile.

He says with joy in his eyes, "No way! That building is owned by the Havishams?"

I say, "Yup!"

"I couldn't possibly not pay rent! I insist on it, Estella!"

I tell him vehemently, "Absolutely not! I stayed out of your client list and now I find out that you are interested in my building, so this is the least I can do!"

He wisely lets it go and comes over and plants a kiss on my forehead and says, "Thank you!"

Chapter 14

The following day, I'm quite busy making sure everything is looked after before our trip. I realize I need another personal assistant because I think I over work poor Cassandra as is! I quickly message Cassandra to hire someone in my absence. She is the best person to find another assistant for me because she knows me like no other.

I get as much done as I can on a Friday afternoon, then I head out to pick up James. We plan on leaving tonight because it will help our jet lag. Mrs. Anderson has packed some of my personal belongings because I was held up at the office so long today that I didn't get a chance to go home. The chateau in France has stuff for me too.

James gets into the car and we head to the airport; thankfully we do not need to be bothered by checking into a public airport. We are flying with the Havishams' jet and Captain Williams is there to greet us.

He has been with the Havishams for decades. He's very kind and profession. I decide on taking the Havisham's jet because Darcy must fly to Mexico to conclude a deal we have been working on.

Captain Williams graciously welcomes us with a relatively new co-pilot, Mr. Steve Tannin. The jet is huge and luxuriously done. It's all mahogany wood on the interior with the finest leather. It's quite big as well; only the best for the Havishams.

The attendant is Chantel, she is tall, blond and very attractive. Of course, Adela loves surrounding herself with beauties. She greets us warmly. I take James for a quick tour before leaving him at the cock pit with Captain Williams. I then head to the primary suite.

I wash my face and slip into this lacy lingerie. As James approaches the bedroom, I tell him to lock the door. I then start kissing him and caressing his crotch. I ask him to take off all his clothing. He obliges. Captain Williams come on the PA and announces that we are about to take off. I tell James to strap into the chair beside the bed, then I strap into the chair beside the window. He looks hesitantly at me because he's naked, so I tell him, "It's OK, no one will come in, just strap in." We take off. I say to James, "My favourite is taking off and landing." He looks at me with wonderment.

After ten minutes of ascent, I un-strap myself and walk over to James and undo his buckle. He's so hot with his rock-hard abs and a beautiful penis. I kneel before him and start sucking him, and his penis just springs to life. He tastes so yummy. I move up to his belly then to his chest. I whisper softly into his ear, "It's your turn. I'm all yours!" He throws me onto the bed and start kissing me hard and passionately. Then he pulls the bra from my left breast and start sucking on my nipple. He nibbles it and moves lower kissing my stomach and working his way to my inner thighs. I feel a sensational tingle inside me. I push my pelvis up against him and open my legs wider.

"I want you so badly," I moan to him. He puts his fingers inside me then licks them.

He says, "Yum." Then he begins licking me. I'm so wet, and he goes faster and faster. I explode in his mouth and scream out loud.

I say to him, "I want you inside me now". He obliges and slides his throbbing penis inside me. He begins pumping me hard and strong. It feels like ecstasy. As he comes, he moans my name and then sinks on top of me. It is an extraordinary feeling having sex six miles in the sky!

We spend the next hour chatting about Paris and Nice warp up in each other arms. Then James brings up a point of tension for him, "I'm still unsure how I feel about going to that chateau where you spent your childhood. I mean you were practically abused there!"

I pull myself up to face him and reiterate with a weary smile on my face, "I love that chateau. I wasn't abused there. I was taken to brothels elsewhere. The house itself has beautiful memories for me which I would like to share with you." He smiles at me and wraps me in his arms.

I wake up with a start. We are still thousands of feet in the air. I untangle myself from James and go into the ensuite for a quick shower. I then head out leaving James to get some rest. I find Chantel, who quickly asks, "Ms. Havisham would you and Mr. Donaldson like some Dom Perignon and some caviar? Or would you rather a larger meal? We have Salmon or chicken with a quinoa salad?"

I tell her, "Smaller for now and if we are still hungry, we will let you know."

I then go to check on Captain Williams and his crew. I haven't flown in this jet for quite some time now. Captain Williams shows me our flight route and schedule. I then go to the main cabin and start up my laptop and check my emails and contact my VP and Cassandra. Everything is well so far.

Just as I was putting away my laptop James enters the main cabin looking all refreshed and beautiful. He's now wearing a polo shirt and casual kakis.

"Hi, how was your nap?"

He responds with, "you let me sleep in!"

I tell him with a cheeky smile, "Of course, you will need your energy for the trip. Here's our itinerary. Tonight, we have the charity event, tomorrow we can sight see and in two days we have the private Versace show, and Thursday through to Monday the chateau in Nice!"

He says, "Sounds great! I'm looking forward to all of it!" Our caviar and champagne come, and we eat and chat about the trip.

The disembark process is a breeze and Pierre ushers us into the Mercedes he acquires in Paris. James is fascinated by the wonderment of the lights, people and architecture. He's never been to Europe and I'm happy I'm sharing this with him. The pandemic also paused some of my travelling to Europe, so it has been a while since I was here.

We pull up to the Ritz Paris and go to the concierge desk, where in French I greet the receptionist and ask for our room. We are quickly helped up to the presidential suite. I've always booked with this hotel, simply because it's the best in Paris and they know me well.

Our room is massive with a beautiful view of the city. James is so impressed by all this. He wants to explore right away. I ask him, "Are you sure you are not tired? We have the ball tonight. If you want, we can take a nap and explore later?"

He says quite enthusiastically, "No, no. Well, if you are tired, we can rest, but if not, I'd like to see the city please. Plus, I got some sleep in the jet."

I smile at his boyish curiosity and say, "I'm use to travelling, so not tired at all. Let's go!" I quickly message Pierre as we enter the lobby, and he pulls up right outside.

In the car I tell James we will do Arch du Triumph today then go for lunch at a little cafe just down the lane. At the Arch James, embarrassingly, takes selfies of us and makes me feel like a tourist for the first time in Paris. I laughingly saying, "I don't think I've ever taken a selfie here!" We both laugh and enjoy being tourists.

We head to the little cafe and it's so cute and quaint, James readily falls in love with it. We get a table outside because it's such a beautiful day. I sip red wine, while James has a Stella Artois. We eat some lunch and then take a stroll. The waitresses and patrons in Paris, like New York, stare at James and I.

At the hotel, James cannot help himself but express how enamoured he is with Paris! I love it. I convince him to nap a bit before the ball. I spend the next hour or so cranking out emails to my clients, Cassandra and my VP.

Around 5pm Paris time, James gets up and I urge him to get ready for our gala. I also presented him with a little gift I picked up last week. It's a Versace tux I got for him for this event. When James sees it, he says, "We bought one last week. I already have an outfit, Estella!"

I tell him, "I know, but I change my mind on that and I'm wearing Versace so this will compliment me." I end off with a huge smile. James doesn't argue with me, he just says thank you, takes it and gets dressed. Plan completed and successful!

Apart from Tom, James will be the second man I have taken to public events as my date. I'm surprisingly not at all nervous about this. I find that James' presence alone brings me inner peace. I'm able to think rationally when he's around. A makeup team comes to do my makeup and hair. Then I quickly slip on my Versace dress. It is black and gold with partly see-through areas. It fits me like a glove. James trots in with his tuxedo… and he looks very handsome. I put a few finishing touches on him and straighten his tie. He looks at me with joy and happiness in his eyes, and says, "You look like a movie star."

I giggle and say, "You look like my leading man. We have to go… we are running late." I am not big on compliments, so I would say anything to change the topic. We head out to the lobby.

The gala is huge, and Pierre arranged a stretch limo for the evening. As we step out of the limo onto the red carpet a furry of flashes hit us. It's blinding and I squeeze James' hand, and he looks at me with comfort. Reporters are asking a million questions about the identity of James, and finally I tell the London Globe Reporter, "He's my date!" I leave it at that and direct James into the gala.

He says to me once we are inside safely away from the paparazzi, "That was not what I expected. That was nuts!"

I tell him reassuringly, "That's the worst of it. Now you can relax and have fun!"

I introduce James to a few dignitaries from Europe, North America and Africa. Although, I don't attend this gala every year, I know a lot of these people because the Havishams have been donating for decades to this specific cause. Every year the gala moves to different exotic locations.

The prime Minister of England and Canada are here, also the Vice President of the US. James is floored by all these people. Along with dignitaries, lots of celebrities are also present, some of which I do not know. Before dinner begins, James is shocked to hear the host calling upon me to give a brief address. I go up, as I've done in the past and urge these patrons to donate in order to provide education, water, food and a basic standard of living to everyone on this earth. I later tell James the Havishams have donated one million this year alone from our US tributary.

The night goes by beautifully, but quickly. James had me on the dance floor for about fifty percent of the time. I don't recall ever having so much fun at these events. I also made sure to speak to a few of my clients and potential clients that are in attendance.

A mutual friend of Tom and myself comes up to me when James was discussing politics with the president of Nairobi. She is an old family acquaintance. "Hi Debra, how are you?" I say as she approaches.

"My dear, Estella! You look so well. Congratulations by the way on the takeover. I think this unofficially makes you one of the richest woman on earth!"

I tell her, "Hardly, but it does come with a lot of responsibility!"

She continues, "Well, at least you are making time for your personal life. Who is he?"

None of your business I want to say but instead, "My date. Would you please excuse me I need to speak to that gentleman!" I point to some random person as I walk away, leaving her standing with her mouth open. I don't care what they think or what gets back to Tom! Or even Adela for that matter.

James and I dance the night away, then find Pierre to take us home. I fall asleep in the car and to my surprise James fetches me into the hotel. Its three a.m. and I'm too exhausted to budge. In our room I think he undressed me and himself then put me into bed.

Chapter 15

I sleep and sleep, it seems like for an eternity. I finally wake up to find James getting breakfast prepared. He sits beside me then kisses my forehead. "Good morning sleeping beauty!" Fuck what time is it? I am startled and James says, "Its two p.m. Don't worry, we are in no rush!"

I begin with, "But the itinerary. We should be in the marketplace now." My need to micromanage is failing.

James says, "We can skip that. Or change it. Don't worry about time. I want you to relax!"

I start with, "But."

Only to be cut off with, "Thank you for last night. I met some inspirational people and I want to donate to this worthy cause!"

I look at him peevishly and say, "I have donated for both of us!" James continues to insist about donating, and I tell him when we get home, he can make a deposit. I am a little taken back about my sleep in and totally screwing up the itinerary, but I don't care anymore, I am just happy to be with this man.

We shower together and enjoy some bantering and cuddling as we look through some of the pictures on his phone (the selfies).

We then head down to Pierre and he takes us for a drive around the city. We get out next to the Eiffel Tower and find a restaurant to have dinner. On Wednesday, we venture out the fashion show. James is nervous because this is not his thing but he is kind enough to feign approval and enjoyment. We meet the designer after and then head out for dinner at my favourite Parisian restaurant.

At dinner we talk about our trip to Nice in a few days. I express to him my enthusiasm about going there, and I notice that he's coming around to the idea that it's not a negative place. We then talk about Washington and his family. He says, "My parents are looking forward to meeting you!"

I ask a little embarrassed, "They know who I am?"

He looks at me peevishly and say, "No, I didn't divulge your name, because my dad might recognize it. I just refer to you as my special girl!" And he winks at me! I don't know how to respond to this as the uneasiness about meeting his family resurfaces. I am quiet on the subject, until my phones buzzes and I pull it out happy for the distraction only to find it's a message from Adela! She knows I'm in France! I excuse myself from my seat, and quickly check my message. She says that not only is her brother been harassing her, but Tom has been trying to contact her. I go back to James at the table and tell him about my message.

"I'm afraid that she is not well, and these people are really annoying her." I tell James.

He says a bit cold heartedly, "I'm sure she is capable of dealing with them."

But that's just it, I tell him, "She is not really dealing with them. She is locked away at home refusing to speak to any of these people. And they just keep harassing her. She is old, they should back off." I'm resolved when I get home, I'll tell both parties to leave her alone. I tell James this, and he doesn't really see it as a good idea but says if I feel I need to do it, then he supports me.

We talk about happier subjects then head back to the hotel for some much-needed rest.

The following day James and I enjoy the busy city of Paris. We also get a chance to catch up on sleep before we make our way to Nice. It's about a nine-hour drive and we both decide to catch up on work. We take the major autoroutes, but I ask Pierre to get off and take us for a scenic drive. Although it will add time to our journey, it is well worth it. The French countryside is breadth taking, so I ask Pierre to pull over. I just want to breadth in the fresh air! James loves the landscape and the tranquillity of the place. He snaps some pictures, and we continue on our way.

When we arrive at the country chateau located a few miles outside of Nice in the village of Gourdon. The town itself has wonderful views because of its elevation. There are many beautiful medieval architectures dating as far back to the 9th century. James loves this history as I quickly give him a brief description of this town.

A few minutes later, we are pulling up to the chateau and it as picturesque as I remember it. It is grand with a long driveway. There is a mote around the property, and as a child I pictured this place as my castle. The roundabout closer to the front entrance is beautifully landscaped and the gardens at the front of the house is in full bloom. Pierre helps us out of the SUV, then goes to get our bags. I run up to the front door and like an ardent child start pressing the button several times. I always do this when I come here. Although they are expecting us, I never gave them a specific day. This chateau is staffed fully year-round as well.

Mrs. Bovary answers the door, and when she sees who it is, she throws up her hands and hugs me. We talk in French, then I switch to English to introduce James to her.

"Monsieur, welcome! You are more beautiful than I imagine et ma petite chere has grown up," she expresses to James and I. Pierre hugs and kisses her too. She practically raised me during the summer months when I visited before. Like Berta, she is a very dear lady to my heart.

We get settled into the house and I take James for a tour of the lovely, crafted chateau. He's devoured by the history, architecture of the house and the grand magnitude of this French castle.

The chateau has been in the Havisham family for two centuries. It was built as a summer home for a French Monarchy in the early 1500s, who have some familial lineage to the Havishams. Over the years it has been restored to its original beauty, but the inside has been modernized to the taste and convenience of today's standards.

James also meets Mr. Champlain, the grounds keeper and Ms. Neil, another housekeeper.

As we get settled into our room, I kiss James behind his neck and whisper, "What do you think now? Is it really a vile dungeon that Adela trapped me in?"

He turns me around to face him and looks into my eyes and says, "It's not a dungeon. It's beautiful; this whole trip has surpassed my expectations!" My heart lights up at this and we begin kissing passionately. We hurriedly take off each other's clothing wanting to feel our naked bodies pressing against each other.

I love his skin on mine. He gently places me on the bed and starts kissing me all over. It tickles but feels so right. He puts himself inside me and gently goes in and out, then faster and faster. I build and I feel him building too; we both orgasm together, whispering each other's name as we come. We cuddle after without saying anything, just savouring this moment.

After showering and dressing in formal attire we head down to the dining room. This room is meant for *Queens* and *Kings* with lavish tones and an ornate ceiling. James thinks I'm being silly because I insist on dressing up and he's a bit uneasy that there is always someone catering to our every needs.

However, I tell him, "Darling, get used to it. I'm a busy person and unfortunately, I don't have time to cook or clean my houses," I say in a matter-of-fact sort of way.

He continues, "Well, I have never been served by others hand and foot. So, it's a bit uncomfortable. And this easy access to travel and rubbing shoulders with anyone you want is weird for me."

I reassure him by saying, "You will get used to it with time." I smile at him. Then Ms. Neil comes in with our first course. We have a five-course meal fit for royalty. After dinner, we retire to the drawing room.

I arrange a pianist to come and play some of my favourite overtures and preludes for this evening. We sit and sip some cognac while being serenade with the wonderful tones of Bach, Vivaldi, Chopin and Beethoven. I thought James might not enjoy this serenade, but as I look over, he's wrapped into the music.

Later, at dusk I take him for a stroll in the lavish gardens. We sit under a canopy and enjoy the refreshing breeze and calming air. James begins with, "This is all very lovely. And now I have second thoughts of you seeing my childhood home." I'm confused, but before I can say anything he continues, "You are very rich, and my family is an ordinary middle-class family. We don't go to Paris every summer to our chateau or attend galas around the world. We don't own a private jet or have a driver or any servants! My family have always worked hard and my parents provided us with a decent life. So, when we travel there next month, you will not see a French maid or a butler!"

OK, I get it. I tell him, "Look I was raised with all this, yes! But I'm not stupid. I know what an average life is. I have volunteered at shelters and been to poor areas around the world. I have seen poverty like you can't imagine. So, I might have luxury, but I hope that doesn't define me. Also, you should know for the first six years of my life my so-called grandfather and his family lived with us until Adela had enough of them and told him to leave. For those six years they treated me like the help. Although Adela always tried her best to protect me from them, she was not around all the time. I felt like an outsider with Arthur and his children. And, I spent a lot of my time with Berta and the other servants. Berta introduced me to church." I pause as I realize I never, not even to Adela, talk about this. I continue, "So money and this doesn't make a person, it is what's inside that person. I care about you because you are a good, gentle man. Adela, regardless of her scorn of mankind, has also taught me to be kind and respectful to everyone, especially to those who are not as fortunate as her." I stop as tears are in my eyes.

I look at him, he wraps his arms around me and says, "I am sorry. I didn't mean to imply."

I stop him and say, "I know what you are getting at. Don't ever be embarrassed of where you came from. You have a loving family. I had none except for a fucked up maternal figure. I would trade all the riches in the world for a loving mother and father like you have!" I stop as tears pour out of me. He holds onto me and kisses them away.

I break out of his arms and tell him I'll be upstairs. He tries to follow me, and I say, "I'm sorry, James. I just need some time alone." I leave him sitting under a yew tree, looking despondently at me.

Chapter 16

I wake up alone in Adela's room the next morning. I went there after I left James and must have fallen asleep. It's quite stuffy and dark in the room. I collect myself and head to my room. I see James standing by the window deep in thought. I say, "Hi, I missed you!" I really did.

He looks at me visibly upset and says, "I fucked up, didn't I. I'm sorry, I didn't mean to upset you!"

I quickly correct him, "No, you didn't fuck up. I have never spoken about not having a mother or father, and I just got a little emotional."

I stop myself as he says, "Thank you for letting me in."

I smile at him and wanting to change subject I say, "You are welcome. Now, I don't want to sleep apart from you ever again. So can you consider just moving in with me?" He looks confused.

"Are you sure?" he finally asks. Am I sure though? This is a huge step for me! But no one has made me feel this way. I couldn't stand the presence of Tom at our house and my other relationships; I couldn't wait for them to leave. James has been the only man that consistently make me want to spend every second of my life with him. I have become a nicer and better version of me when he's around. I'm simply happy with him.

I tell him, "Yes, absolutely!" I truly mean this.

He looks at me and holds my hand then says, "OK, but on a trial run. If it gets too overwhelming, we can always go back to our mutual places." OK sounds fair,

I concede, "OK, sounds good—maybe you will want to run away from me!"

He looks at me with his boyish smile and says, "Never!"

An idea just entered my thought – "Would you like me to take you to a brothel?"

James looks at me stunned, then says dryly, "No, thank you". OK so that's not his thing, don't judge me!

I tell him, "OK." I thought it would be wickedly fun, but clearly not his thing.

Later that day, I gave James a real tour of the chateau explaining the architectural and the actual history of the place. I take James with the help of Mr. Champlain around the vast property. I then leave James to do a sketch of one of the ponds. I go back the main house and chat with Madame Bovary and some of the other housekeepers. I really love this place.

For the next couple of days, we spend time at the chateau and I also get Pierre to drive us into the city of Nice. James and I explore all the wonderments of this beautiful city. We also indulge in some amazing French cuisine at a few of the restaurants. The whole trip has exceeded my expectation. I love rediscovering my childhood summer home with James.

The day before we depart we go for a bike ride in the fields then head off to a small town about six km from the house. The countryside is so peaceful and picturesque. We stop at a meadow before the market to just smell the flowers and frolic in the sun.

James holds me tight and kisses me passionately. I look at him and unzip his pants, then I hike my skirt up to my pelvis. He fingers my panties and says, "My Ms. Havishams you are very wet!" He then pushes my panties to the side and slides himself inside me. It feels magical! He lays me down on a bed of grass and summer blooms. His penis fills me up as he moves faster and faster. I am about to come when he says, "Wait for me." I can't stand it any long and I explode around him and he does the same. We both exhale each other's names.

We lay in the grass for some time, just staring at the clouds. I say, "Can we move here? This trip has surpassed my expectations."

He says with mirth in his voice, "Yes, we can someday, but no brothels." I can't help but laugh. We collect ourselves and fix our appearances then head to the small village.

It's a cute bustling site with fresh produce everywhere to be seen. I buy some steak, mushrooms and veggies. I want to make dinner tonight before we head home. I love this market because they only use the freshest and naturally grown produce. James feels a bit lost as most of the merchants are French speaking, unlike Paris and Nice, but I'm there to translate for him.

We head back and I let James go up and get ready for dinner, while I prepare the meat and vegetables. Madame Bovary helps me to finish up, while I go up to get showered and changed.

We dine in the garden terrace. It's seven p.m. and at three a.m. Pierre will be ready to take us to the jet. I don't want to leave. Although it was a short trip, I love every minute of it. It was truly stress free. I didn't think about work, Adela, or her brother or even Tom. I just took this trip moment by moment. There was no three a.m. wake up or no panicking for air. I love being in James' company and importantly I did not once think it was wrong to be happy!

After dinner, which I made perfectly—the steak was a nice medium rare—we head to the kitchen to say our goodbyes to my dear staff. I hug Madame Bovary and kiss her twice before going to our room to pack. I need to find time to come to this place more often.

During our car ride to the tarmac, we are both very quiet. I think we are thinking about tomorrow and going back to work and dealing with all the hassles that come with that, at least that is what my mind is drifting to. I break the silence by saying, "I am looking forward to meeting your family in a few weeks!"

He looks at me and smile, then kisses me gently and whispers, "Me too."

We board the plane, and we are both a little sad leaving France. Tomorrow will be insane because I have scheduled two important meetings I cannot miss. In the plane we buckle ourselves, then I notice James drifting off to sleep as we take off and I too, fall asleep.

Chapter 17

The first meeting goes better than expected. Our telecommunication network is expanding thanks to rubbing shoulders with a Malaysian dignitary in Paris. I have another meeting schedule at two, but I feel quite tired. So, I leave to get some air and a coffee.

As I am walking in the street, I hear someone calling my name. I turn around and almost fall onto Tom Calloway! What the fuck!

He says, "Hi, Estella! I've been waiting for you!" No, no, no.

I say, "Hi, Tom. Why? What do you want?"

He continues, "Can we sit down, please?"

I tell him, "I can't right now. I have a meeting in twenty minutes, can we do this after. I need to go. Come to my office around four p.m." As I tell him this I quickly message Pierre who is waiting for me double parked in a spot. Thank heavens he's here. I quickly go into the car for the five-minute drive.

At four, after my meeting, Tom is waiting in the lobby. I see him through my glass doors. He looks good, like a senator, so what does he want with me? I need this to stop now; it cannot be prolonged.

After Tom moved to California, he pursued a career in politics. He became a senator last year and then married his southern bell. I thought he had his life together both personally and professionally. I just don't understand why he is insisting on contacting me.

I step out onto the lobby and usher Tom into my office. He says, "Nice office, Ms. CEO!" Cut the small talk and get to the chase because I'm busy—

I want to say to him, but instead I smile and say, "Thanks. What's going on Tom?"

"Well, I miss you. It's that simple," he says.

I respond with, "Tom, you are newly married with a career you always wanted. Why in God's name would you miss me?"

He continues, "We had a very special connection, and no one can replace that. I tried moving on with Cindy and before her other women. But I always come back to wanting you. Don't you feel it, Estella? I still love you and want you in my life. We can be a powerhouse together!" He pauses. I sit quietly on the corner of my desk. I know this man very well. He's choosing his words wisely.

I do fear him because he is a type A personality. He gets what he wants. I can control him and make him submissive in the bedroom and to some extent in the public realm, but I need to be in a relationship with him to have that kind of control over him. I need to use sex. I obviously cannot nor do I desire to at this point. So, I do not have any control over him and he might do something stupid and unpredictable. I need to outsmart him and be two steps ahead of him.

I let him continue, "You give me a reason to live."

That's an extreme statement, so I interrupt; "Tom, that's not true. Cindy has been great for you. Your family likes her and she is just what you need. You need a sub, not a dominant. You are the dominant."

He says, "I thought a good sub would suffice, but I'm bored of her. I don't want another 'dom' either, I only want you." At that point he pulls out a leather strap I used to put around his neck and he throws it on my desk. Then he says, "I'm all yours."

"I do not want a relationship with you any more. So, that's not an option." I say as simply as I can gesture it.

He responds with, "Because of James Donaldson! Fuck him! He's a loser, not a real man. He's not your type, anyways. You are just wasting your time with him. You need me." Then he passionately throws himself in one of my wing tip chairs.

I tell him in a calm and collective voice, "It's not because of him. He has nothing to do with this. It's us, we are divorced. We had our chance, and it didn't work out. I don't feel the same as you. This ends here."

He puts his head in his arms and says in an animalistic groan or cry, "You cannot leave me. I need you. You are my rock. I don't want to live without you." He gets up and in a fury goes to the window, then turns to face me. There is rage in his eyes as he says, "It's all his fault. It's him." He comes to me and grabs my hands. "Can't you understand how much I need you?" He's wild and venomous. He continues, "He's not right for you. He's not even your type. He's weak and a loser. You need a man like me. I can take you to the top, baby. Just you and I. We can accomplish so much." I don't know if I'm mad at his macho bullshit or the fact he's hurting my wrists.

I say, "Tom, let go of me!" He quickly realizes the pressure he has on me and let's go.

Then goes on his knees and says, "I'm all yours, do whatever you want to me. I'm your servant!"

I step back and say, "Tom, we don't have that type of relationship any more. We do not have any sort of relationship. Don't ever contact me again." I then press the speaker for Cassandra and say, "Mr. Calloway is leaving now." She knows to get security.

He gets up and steps back, someone knocks at the door then comes in. It's Pierre, ready to escort Tom out. He leaves quietly, and I sink down into my chair. Cassandra pokes her head in and asks if I'm OK. I say, "Better now, thanks. Can you close the door please?" I need to be alone. I didn't realize Tom will be an issue; he is jealous of James, and he just can't take no for an answer, that's the problem.

In the morning I send a deterrent letter with Pierre to Tom at the hotel he's staying. I send him a note saying, "Back off, we are over. Do not contact me again." And two pictures of him tied up naked. It's petty but I'm out of options with this man. He's a fucking senator so this should persuade him to leave me alone. In the back of my mind, I know this might be futile and would end up hurting me more. But I'm out of options.

I don't share this with James. We are still getting over our high from France. This week has been busy for both of us but every night we have been spending together. On the weekend we plan on moving him into my place.

The week passes by without any other excitements. On Friday, Pierre escorts me to the SUV then we head over to get James. I see him walking down the escalator then he exits the building and walk toward the car. He enters and says, "Hi baby, I've missed you all day!" This puts a smile on my face, and I nozzle into him.

At his place we get a few more items he will need for the week. Tomorrow professional movers will pack his clothing, toiletries and other essentials to my place. He plans on keeping the loft for a bit. But I am looking into purchasing the building.

We head back to my place and Felix has prepared a beautiful roasted Cornish hen with balsamic vinaigrette salad. I, as per my usual, pick at my meal. James has noticed my demur look since Tom came to my office but has said nothing all week. He says, "So, what's going on? And tell me everything because I know something is clearly bothering you! Is it the move?"

I breathe in then say, "No, the move has actually lifted my spirits. It's Tom, after we got back he came and unexpectedly stormed into my office and basically demanded that I take him back. I, of course, said I have no interest, but he was being persistent. So, Pierre pretty much threw him out." I pause to see James take a deep breath.

I continue, "I think he's not taking no for an answer." I pause again to sigh and say quickly, "And the next day I sent Pierre with some not so nice pictures and a note saying back off." I end. At this last part James looks at me with a fiery intensity in his eyes.

He says calmly, "That was stupid. You are just aggravating the situation." He pauses then says, "I think I should have a word with him now. This has gone on too long!" No, bad idea.

I say, "I don't think that would be good. I know Tom very well and that will really aggravate him."

James continues, "Then what do you want to do? Another option is contacting the authorities? Maybe getting a restraining order?"

I thought of that too, and I say, "No. I don't want anything leaking to the media. I'll handle it for now. Plus, I'm not afraid of him. I have a team of people always around me." I don't feel I have this situation under control, but what else can I do?

"OK but you have to promise me no more private meetings with this man. And if he insists on harassing you, I'll call the cops. I'm not risking anything with you!" James proclaims. A bit macho, but I back down. I have no better solutions anyways.

Our weekend is filled with unpacking James' stuff and packing our stuff for the Washington trip. As time gets closer for the departure date, I get more nervous, but don't mention anything to James.

Saturday evening we go out to a new restaurant in the city and we are treated to a tasting menu prepared by a well-known Italian chef. It's delicious and James comments, "I can never get use to all this."

I ask, "What?"

He says, "You know the jet, the fancy restaurants and especially the paparazzi. They are insane."

I laugh, then reply, "No one gets use to them! I hate being photographed. So, I avoid it at all chance."

He continues, "But you are always on page six or in those tabloids!"

I give him a look with my head cock to one side, and I say, "you read page six and the tabloids?"

He smiles and says, "When you are dating the most eligible bachelorette in the US, everyone tells you what's in the papers!"

I look at him and sadly say, "It's a lifestyle that has its pros and cons. After a while it can become dull."

I then ask him quickly, "Does your family now know who you are dating?" I didn't want them to know initially but I don't think I care any more.

He says, "I didn't mention your name, but we are getting a lot of media attention, so there is a possibility. Is that OK?"

I say, "Ohh, I don't care if they know who I am. They will eventually!"

We talk more about work and our impending trip. Then we go for a stroll in Central Park. I have a weird craving for gelato, and I make James take me to an ice cream shop. He's never tasted gelato and has no interest in it, so he gets a huge ice cream cone and I get the smallest scope of gelato in a huge waffle cone.

We continue to talk and enjoy the refreshing breeze of the night. Then we head back to the SUV. James says out of nowhere, "Were people following us?"

I look at him and say, "Yes, I hired a personal bodyguard." And a minute later I say, "I think it would be a good idea for you to have a bodyguard as well. Tom can be dangerous and unpredictable."

He says, "When were you going to tell me this?"

I say, "At dinner, but it honestly just slipped out of my mind! So can you accept the bodyguard please?"

He looks at me with I think anger in his eyes, "No, absolutely not! I do not need a bodyguard and I'm certainly not afraid of a confrontation with Mr. Calloway!" He's being too macho again. This is for his protection.

I plead with him, "Listen, I know this man very well and he's prone to violent behaviour."

He cuts me off and says frantically, "Did he hurt you?"

I look at him with a playful smile and say, "Of course not. But I think he's desperate and he owns a gun. I'm afraid he might hurt himself or one, if not both of us. I know how his mind works. That would not be above him!"

This is extreme but I like to consider all possibilities. I like full control and no surprises.

I continue with genuine pleads in my tone, "James, I know this man and after deducing all possibilities I would have peace of mind if you agreed to this... please!"

He looks at me and says, "How intrusive will this be?"

I tell him, "Not at all. I had a guard on us since Tom came to my office on Tuesday and you noticed him today... Saturday." With that he agrees but warns that it cannot be intrusive to his life.

The weekend goes exceptionally well. On Sunday we traverse the finger lake region again and go antique shopping. At lunch James says, "Something is kinda bugging me about us."

I say, "What's that darling?"

He continues, "Well, it's this lifestyle. I'm still not comfortable with it. I mean I feel a bit emasculated by you and by us!"

I look at him and say, "I am very successful and have more than the average person. So, don't feel emasculated. You are a nice person with qualities I enjoy."

He looks at me and says, "It really bugs me that you pay for everything. I'm all about equality, but we are not equals at all in this relationship."

I look at him, and say, "What's bugging you? If the roles were reverse, you won't have a problem paying for everything. But because I'm the woman, you feel unequal! Look I like expensive things and I have the means of getting them. So just enjoy my company, please!" I stop, I don't want to talk about money. He senses that this conversation is annoying me and backs off.

I know the money thing is an issue for him and he's not used to having domestic help, drivers and basically everything at his fingertips, but that's part of who I am. I tell him, "I know this is uncomfortable for you. But this is my life. This is who I am—so please don't feel that way. Don't be uncomfortable with my lifestyle."

We end it at that, but I know it still bothers him to constantly be catered to but I'm not going to apologize for who I am. I work hard for everything I have, so I am not going to feel bad because I don't need to depend on a man for his protection or finance.

Chapter 18

Monday morning, I schedule another meeting with Mr. Yamamoto. He wants to purchase my company and expand it into the Japanese market. He knows about my acquisition of the Havisham development company and has pitched me an offer for my telecommunication company. I don't know how I feel about this, but what he's offering is astronomical. The only problem is I'll be losing my baby.

As it stands, I cannot just sell. I started this company from scratch. I built it to what it is today. Although he's willing to pay over market value for it, in two years it is estimated to be worth more if I keep making it a dominant and competitive corporation.

But there is also the restate company I just inherited. I was groomed to run that company and it is sort of my legacy. As we speak someone else I just hired is running it with a board of directors. I'm sure they are all capable, but they are still stagnant. I can do so much with that company to make it an international phenomenon. That would of course take time and energy, which I don't have right now!

I feel a bit guilty not pouring my heart and soul into the Havisham company. I think right now I'm going to make Mr. Yamamoto salivate for my company.

***

My meeting goes exceptionally well. I have him eating out of my hand. He desperately wants my company and is willing to pay a lot for it. But I'm still holding onto it for now.

It's two p.m. and I want to clear my head, so I go for a walk. It's blistering hot outside. I message James, "I'm thinking of you." I know he's in court today, so I know he will not respond right away.

My life has really changed with him. I can't believe I'm capable of having a normal relationship with someone. I mean I'm not using him for just sex, nor do I want to inflict pain on him. I just want him to be happy and for us to be happy together.

If you want to put a label on it, yes he's my boyfriend, although, that sounds so juvenile. He has a kind soul and a heart. He's genuinely a good person who always try to do the right thing. I am learning how to be a better person by being around him.

Tonight, we are meeting at a nice French restaurant in the city. I can't wait to see him. I have been longing to feel him all day.

I return to the office, completely forgetting to eat lunch of course. I check some more files and notice that James has responded. I decide it's time to wrap stuff up and head home to change. I message James to meet at the restaurant.

At dinner we chat about our day and I order the wine, I say to the waitress, "Can you please bring me a bottle of the 2005 Vieux Chateau certain." I love this wine! James is now taking a small interest in wine although he still thinks it is gross. He orders a beer.

After I order my wine, he says, "I hope you know that you are one of the nicest persons I know." I am a bit surprise by this comment.

I look at him and say, "Really?"

He says, "You treat people with respect. You are a not snobby. I know a few 'rich' people who are disgustingly rude to servers and people they think are below them. That's not you." I don't care for compliments, but I like this one. I always viewed myself as a cold person to everyone, always in a rush but nevertheless will always say please and thank you to everyone. Plus, how I treated Philip will always haunt me. I have not shared this past with James because it is dead and buried, but Philip was a nice person just like James. I can excuse my behaviour towards Tom and others like him, but Philip was different. It is part of my past that I cannot forgive myself for.

I tell him, "Thank you, James! That's probably the nicest compliment anyone has given me. Snobby runs in my family like my aunt and uncle, and the whole Havisham clan. I want to be nothing like them!" Hence why I'm dating you! I don't care about your family heritage or pedigree, but I refrain from saying this to him as it's uncouth.

He responds saying, "Well I don't know them, but you are a beautiful person, Ms. Estella Havisham." With that I reach over and kiss his hand.

He continues, "You also treat people that work for you like family, like Pierre, Mrs. Anderson and Madame Bovary."

I stop him, and say, "They practically all raised me." I continue, "As a child, apart from Adela, no one took an interest in me, so I turned to all the staff Adela employed. They opened their home and heart to me. I am very grateful for that, or I might have turned out like my cousins. I also hire people with moral compasses like Cassandra and Darcy." I think about this for a second as my wine and his beer come, and the waitress pours it into my glass. After I look up at her and say, "Thank you." She smiles and scampers away. I never really reflected on the people that have always been in my life, maybe I was never as cold as I thought I was. Certainly, my relationship with James has soften me and my view of the world. I realize at this exact moment that I do not want to end up alone like Adela in this world.

***

Finally, the big day comes for our departure to Washington—and we once again board the Havisham's jet. I decide on this one because mine is tied up with Mr. Darcy. The flight is about four hours and unfortunately, we spend the time doing work.

"I have an important trip to California when we get back. Would you like to come? I must go to Havisham's office in LA to make sure everything is running smoothly and to move a big purchase we just made."

James says, "Next week I'm tied up in court, so I won't be able to accompany you. I'm sorry!" That's too bad because I'll miss him.

"That's OK." I look dower and a bit sad, but I understand busy schedules!

"How long will you be gone for?" he asks, and I say cheekily.

"For about two days. Then I'll head back here on Saturday morning, and we can go out for dinner. There is a production of Swan Lake playing that I wouldn't mind seeing on Saturday. Can you oblige me?"

"Ballet? Umm, well it's not my thing!" Then he says, "But of course, I'll go. How can I possibly say no to you!" I give him one of my big smiles.

We land at Ronald Reagan Washington Airport, then Pierre goes off to get our SUV. As we wait for our ride, I insist on staying at a hotel in the little town of Tacoma because I cannot imagine myself at a stranger's home. I mention this here because I knew he has his heart set on staying at his family's home with me, but that won't do. I won't be comfortable, and James knows this so he doesn't push for it.

The hotel is half decent and the room is spacious enough, but a little subpar to my standards. Although, I tell him it's OK for him to stay with his family, he wants to stay with me, which

I am quite happy about!

We check into the hotel and head up to our room. At six p.m. we will have dinner at his parents' home, where I'll meet them and his sister. I think his aunt and uncle will be joining us too. Although I don't want this to be a big thing, I'm so nervous about it because it's new to me. I haven't really said any of this to James.

I dress in a white, silk summer dress by Dior. It feels comfortable against my skin and it flows well on my thin figure. James looks like the all-American boy. He's wearing khakis and a polo shirt. He looks so yummy that I couldn't help going up to him and nibble on his ear lobe. He looks at me and throws me onto the bed.

I hike up my dress and say, "Come fuck me, Mr. Donaldson." He looks at me with a grin on his face and crawls over. He unzips his pants and his penis springs to life. He fingers me and gently puts himself into my very wet vagina. He's gentle today, and it feels amazing. As his motion increases, I come hard at the same time he does. Then he pulls out and lays beside me.

"Ms. Havisham that's called a quickie!" he says.

I roll over and kiss him then say, "Thanks. I needed that! Now let's go!" I spring off the bed and head to the bathroom. In five minutes we are riding down the elevator and heading towards this childhood home.

James has not seen his parents yet as it's customary for his parents to get him from the airport. However, this time it's a bit different with me.

Their house is tucked away in a quaint neighbourhood. It's exactly as I imagined it—all American. His parents see the SUV pull up and come out to greet us. His mom is around sixty or so and has a very motherly look. She is a retired schoolteacher, and his dad is also a lawyer. She smiles genuinely seeing James and runs out to hug him. His dad, a bit older, is more reserve but goes to his son after and hugs him.

They all then look to me, I say, "It's so nice to meet both of you Mr. and Mrs. Donaldson." I awkwardly put out my hand, but I think I should have hugged them. James quickly introduces me to them, and we hug.

James leads the conversation as we enter the house. He introduces me to his sister saying, "Karen this is my girlfriend, Estella. Be nice!" And he gives her a big hug. She is bouncy and full of life, and the same girl I saw him with in New York.

She comes over and bear hugs me, saying, "It's so good to meet you. You are gorgeous! James, she is really beautiful. She looks like a Barbie!" James starts getting red from embarrassment and so do I.

He quickly says, "Honestly, you are too embarrassing!"

I say, "Thanks I think."

She quickly says, "Ohh, it's a compliment. Sorry for being so forward. But you are really pretty!" I smile at her. I think I might like her.

We continue to chat with his parents. They are very polite. His sister brings out Horderves for us and they are all very hospitable. His mom says, "My dear, I'm so happy you are in James' life. He's told us a little about you, but not much. What do you do?"

I look at her and say, "He's a nice person. I own two companies."

And his dad chimes in saying, "What are they?" I didn't expect to talk about work so soon and I don't really want to.

I am about to answer, when James says, "Companies that you might not have heard about. So, it's irrelevant at this point. Mom, who's coming tonight?"

The mom says, "Aunt Doris and Uncle Glen. Cindy might come too."

I see the name of Cindy has made James a bit tense, so I ask, "Who's Cindy?"

The mom says, "An old friend of the family." That sounds dubious—and I did my homework, but I don't pursue it.

Mr. Donaldson then says, "James, you have to see my new tool shed out back! Let's go and let the women folk talk!" A bit sexist and crass, which I'm not impressed by. But I don't say anything.

James looks over at me and whispers, "Are you OK to be here by yourself?"

Before I can respond Karen says, "We are not going to bite James! Honestly!" With that I smile at him, and he goes.

The women: Mrs. Donaldson seems very motherly and attentive. We talk about the weather and the upcoming birthday. She then says, "I must inquire, why didn't you guys want to stay with us instead of the hotel?"

I tell her, "Ohh, we didn't want to burden you. I know James stays here when he visits, but I didn't want to put you guys out. And it's quite fine. I stay in hotels all the time, so I'm quite comfortable in them."

She continues, "Well if you change your mind, James' room is all yours!" I thank her wholeheartedly for the room.

Karen says, "How's living in New York? And what exactly do you do?" I then decide to explain what I do for a living and share with them my last name. Karen has heard of my telecommunication company and me personally because I have been in the media frequently. Mrs. Donaldson has heard of the Havisham company and the of course the family. She is caught by surprise and says, "I wish James would have told me who you are earlier!"

I quickly say, "That's my fault. I asked him not to because I didn't want to drag attention to myself." The mom smiles at me and we begin chatting about work and travelling. Karen chimes in when any opportunity presented itself to talk about fashion and restaurants. She's a sweetheart but a little bit of a ditz.

When the men come back, we are laughing about something silly Karen said, and drinking Karen's homemade Sangria. I usually don't drink when I first meet people, but I feel nervous because I usually don't do the family thing.

James looks at me and asks, "Are you drinking?"

I giggle at him and say, "Try some. It's delicious." Just at that moment the doorbell rings.

James whispers to me and asks, "Are you sure you are OK?"

I reassure him by saying, "Yup." And I give him a peck on the cheek.

His aunt and uncle arrive bearing a fruit tray and salmon rolls, which almost makes its way onto the floor. They are nice and friendly enough. James pulls me away upstairs to give me a tour and Karen wants to follow but James shoos her away.

His bedroom is very cute and boyish. On one wall a big Baywatch poster is hung and on the other random pictures of periodic table and math equations are strategically placed. He throws me on his bed and I pull him onto me then roll him over and straddle him. I then pin his arm over his head, and say, "I like your mom and sister."

He then says, "That's good. If they are too much, then just come to me." So, he can protect me… that's funny, I smile at him. He continues, "I know you don't need protecting. But I am going to warn you. My ex is coming over. I don't know why, but she is. And you have nothing to worry about. Cindy is an old family friend. We are actually good friends still." I knew this Cindy was the ex-fiancé! Without saying a word, I get off of him, and he can tell I'm not happy.

I finally say, "Why is she coming over? And you are still friends? In what capacity?" My tone alone tells him I'm pissed.

He quickly says, "I have no idea why she is coming. But it's no big deal. She is a nice person, and we were over a long, long time ago. I haven't spoken to her in over a year. So, there is nothing to get worked up over. Please smile and be happy. Don't let this ruin our trip!"

I look at him and say, "I don't like exes. They should not be around. But I am not going to let this interrupt this trip!" I am not a jealous person, but I have never had a relationship like this with anyone either! Right on cue, Mrs. Donaldson is calling us down because dinner is ready.

When we go downstairs Cindy makes her entrance. She is blonde and petit, exactly James' type. I say as politely as I can muster, "Nice to meet you." But what I really wanted to say is get the fuck out of here.

I stay quiet as we take our seats and James holds my hand as we sit down. Karen, oblivious to anyone's mood, rattles on about who I am and asks me a million questions during dinner. I am happy for the distraction as I don't have to make pleasantries with anyone else.

However, I notice that Cindy is making small talk with James from across the table. She is clearly flirting.

Although in the past this sort of silliness would never bother me, James is different. Her presence is really pissing me off!

I notice him trying to curtail his responses to her, but she of course doesn't take the hint. Just when I am about to eat Mr. Donaldson announces, "So Estella, my Karen informed me who you are! Wow, a Havisham in my house! One of the premier families of this country. That's why you were so coy about your profession!"

James interrupts him, "Dad, I don't think Estella wants to discuss that now. So can we drop it!"

Mr. Donaldson looks at his wife and she says, "John, be respectful!" Mr. Donaldson continues, "What did I do? I was just complimenting her!"

I finally say, "It's OK. Yes, I'm a Havisham. I just don't want anyone to make a big deal about it." I smile then we continue dinner.

We go into the family's den. It's a very quaint and an all-American house to me by the all-American family that lives here. Everyone seem stuffed from dinner, even I ate a little too much because I was trying to avoid questions and I figure if my mouth is full then I can't respond.

Karen and Mrs. Donaldson have laid out quite the spread of desserts with coffee, tea and even digestifs. I sit next to Mrs. Donaldson and her sister, Doris Smith. We chat about the latest home decor and trends. I add as much to the conversation as I could. James is chatting with his dad, uncle, Karen and Cindy.

Our eyes constantly meet, he has the 'are you OK look' every time. After ten minutes he comes over to join our conversation. He sits beside me and holds my hand. I don't need his reassurance because I'm quite capable of taking care of myself, but I let him.

Karen then pulls me to the kitchen to show me this dress she has recently purchased for the party. As I am leaving the room, I notice Cindy inching her way closer to James.

Although I am not happy, I do not go back to him right away. I'm not the jealous type but this woman's presence does bother me. I listen to his sister talk more about what she is going to wear, then we emerge back into the den. Everyone is still conversing, and James is talking with Cindy.

I go over. I say, "Hi."

And he looks at me with a concern smile and says, "Hi, I miss you." He then pecks me on the cheek.

Cindy says, "All evening I didn't really get a chance to talk to you, Estella!"

James cuts her off saying, "We have to go unfortunately, maybe another time." I just smile and say nothing.

She then says, "Ohh too bad. But I guess I'll see you guys on Saturday!" She will be at the party!

I say, "Great. Can't wait. Good night." And we go over to his mom and dad to say our goodbyes. Then Karen bear hugs both of us and we say goodbye to his aunt and uncle.

Pierre is patiently outside waiting for us. In the car my smile wears off quickly and is replaced by a frown. He asks, "What's wrong, baby?"

I say, "Why was she there? And what did she have to say to you?"

He breaths in and says, "I don't know why she was there. And she just wanted to know how I was doing. We haven't spoken in a long time, and she wanted to catch up. I know you wouldn't be happy, but I tried to put a distance between us!"

I tell him, "So, she is your friend? I don't understand that sort of relationship. If you have fucked someone you should not be their friend after. I'm not comfortable with her in your life!" I tell him exactly how I feel. I do not hold back! Some would think I'm unreasonable to tell him not to be friends with someone, but I don't like this.

He looks at me with intrigue, possibly anger. He finally says, "I don't like you telling me who I can be friends with. But I understand your point about Cindy being my ex. However, I have known her for fifteen years. I cannot just cut her out of my life, but I am willing to distance myself from her. By the way, I trust you and your interaction with your ex." Of course, I hate Tom, but I know I need to trust him too.

This is a lot for me so I say, "OK, I need to think how I feel about that."

We are silent on the rest of the way to the hotel. When we get to our room, I go to the bathroom for a quick shower. I do not look around for James as he is not in the room when I come out of the shower. I head straight to the bed and fall asleep.

Chapter 19

In the morning, James is spread out beside me. It's six a.m. and I'm restless. I want to go home. I have a million things pending and I'm not comfortable here.

I quietly slip out of bed and go shower and get dress. I then go downstairs to the cafe and pull out my laptop. I am sipping on a latte and shooting out emails when James finds me.

"Good morning," I greet him.

He says, "How did you sleep?"

I respond with, "Well and you?"

He says, "Pretty good. You were up early! And I see working away."

I tell him, "Yes, I'm quite busy at work. I thought I could get a few things done."

There is an uncomfortable and unmistakeable tension between us, then he says, "Well, I hope you can squeeze me in today as I would love to show you around town. You can see where I went to school!" Although this is cute and exciting, all that comes into my mind is—*that was probably where he and Kathy made out! Yuck!*

He knows I'm not happy or in a particularly good mood. He says in his boyish charming way, "I really want you to be happy here. This is a special trip for me as I don't bring girls to meet my parents. So, I really want you to be happy." He goes silent, so I decide to mention the elephant that's in the room.

I say sarcastically, "Why do you have to bring girls here? She already comes to your parents' house." I pause then add, "I'm not quite happy. I'm not particularly impressed by meeting your high school sweetheart that you are still friends with. Do you know why I'm successful with the telecommunications company?"

This throws him by surprise, but he says, "Hard work and intelligence?"

I tell him, "Partially, but more so because I know how people think for the most part. I know what deals to make and when to make them. I know how to read the market. And when I meet with buyers I know exactly how to communicate with them." I pause then continue, "This Cindy still wants you. She is jealous of me and is trying to interject herself between us."

He starts with, "I don't think you are right about her. She has no romantic interest in me…"

I cut him off saying, "You don't see it but I do. Trust me, I'm a 100% sure about this. I'm not the jealous type either. However, this is a big deal for me. Being here, meeting your parents and sister is a huge deal. I have never done the girlfriend thing with Tom, our family knew each other, so there were no introductions or get togethers."

I continue, "Her being here is fucking everything up. I don't share, and this is why I'm irritated. I know she was also your ex-fiancé." It's the complete truth, and I want him to know I know.

He looks at me intensely then says, "Yes, we were engaged when I was really young and stupid. It was all a mistake. I'm sorry I haven't been thinking what this trip really means to you. I know it's a big step for you and trust me it is for me too. And I'm so happy you are here! As for Cindy, she is not important. Yes, she is a friend, but I don't need her in my life. I need and want you. So, if you are asking me to choose, I wholeheartedly choose you, Ms. Havisham." As he says this, he takes my hand and kisses it. I smile at him. I am so fond of this man to the point that he causes me to be jealous! This kinda puts me at ease as he is willing to cut her out of his life.

We decide a change of scenery is in store and he wants me to see his middle and high school. The day is fun, and the historical downtown of city is quaint and lovely.

A young couple stop us in the street to greet James. Brad and Phyllis are their respective names. Phyllis says, "We have heard the rumours about you! How nice to meet you!"

I say, "Likewise. I hope you have heard only good things!"

Brad chimes in saying, "Well, the internet have not done enough justice with regards to your beauty!" This compliment makes me a little uncomfortable as Phyllis doesn't look too please with it. They already know who I am and I guess I shouldn't be surprise because James has been photographed with me many times.

I quickly change topic by saying, "How do you guys know James?"

Phyllis says, "We all went to high school together, ages ago! We hardly get to see this one." Then she gently tucks at him. She continues, "So when we heard he is bringing home a girl, we all got so curious!" I try not to roll my eyes at small town values. But we chat some more about the party! Apparently, they will be there tonight as well.

This is really turning out to be the event as it seems like the whole little town is invited!

James and I continue our stroll into a diner. Not surprising but most of the patrons know James! Some are even related to him! We say our hellos and do the introductions, then we sit down to eat.

I am not snobby, but I don't do diner food. So, I get a coffee and a muffin. He says, "That's all you are having? You need to eat. You are all skin and bones!"

I tell him, "I'm not particularly hungry and there isn't anything on the menu that I would be interested in." I know he would see this as snobbery, but I didn't not care.

Surprisingly he does not chide me but says, "I'm getting the cheeseburger. It's the best I have ever eaten! It's charcoal." Obviously, these are words and concepts are foreign to me as I've never had a cheeseburger! But I smile and nod.

When his order comes, I'm nibbling away on my muffin. It's quite stale so I am just eating the top part. His meal smells heavenly! I tell him, "That smells delicious!"

He says, "Have a bite, try some!"

I tell him, "No, I don't want to impose. I've never had a cheeseburger."

With that he slides over his plate and says, "Dig in!" I take a bite and it's good... melted cheese on ground meat. Not bad at all. Not life altering, but it's good.

I slide back his plate and say, "It's yummy!"

He says, "Have more."

And I tell him, "I think I'll try their apple pie!"

He looks at me dubiously and say, "Dessert?"

I respond, "Yes." Then I smiled.

I have been eating less actual food, and more desserts over the past couple of weeks. I've been craving more sweets, including baked goods. I will need to cut it off soon! I think about this and decide to pass on the apple pie. The cheeseburger bite and my nibbles of muffin have satisfied my appetite.

We first drive by his elementary school. Unfortunately, we couldn't go in but James tells me stories about his time there and he shows me their football field. Then we go to his high school which is a bit bigger. Compared to mine both schools are so tiny. I share some insight about the private schools I attended, and James jestingly says, "now you see how the real world lives!" His comments are true because I just assumed my life is the norm.

We head back to the hotel to get ready for dinner. James goes into shower and I join him. He washes my back and slides his hard naked penis between my legs. He flips me around and spreads my legs. Then he inserts his penis inside me.

It feels magical as he goes faster and faster. We both orgasm together screaming and moaning each other's names as we come.

He dries me after and picks me up from the bathroom and takes me to the bed. There we lay down together. He kisses my hand and says, "Ms. Havisham, I'm quite fond of you." I smile slightly but don't respond. He goes on, "I think we make a good couple."

I say, "Yes, we do. I'm happy!"

He smiles broadly and says, "I think I've fallen in love with you!" Fuck! I was afraid of this.

A sense of fear crosses my face, then I visible breath in and say, "What time is our dinner reservation?" Then I am frozen in the bed, as I do not know what to say or do! I knew this was coming but I did not prepare myself to respond to him.

He goes on, "Don't panic. You don't need to say anything. I wanted to say this to you a while ago but I was afraid of pushing you away."

I don't know what to think, so I say, "OK." Then I smile.

I roll off the bed and head back into the bathroom to get dress. I don't want to show him my panic. What am I doing with this guy? I will hurt him! My mind races to the fact that this is exactly what Adela has groomed me to do.

I don't want to hurt him, but I cannot love him. I enjoy his company, but that doesn't mean I love him! I might not feel the same next week or next month! I need a break. I need to end this, to continue this will make him think I love him back and *I don't.*

I need to cut my loses; I'll miss him though. I need to put an end to this, but not here, not now. After, yes back in New York I'll end things. Fuck, a million things are rushing through my mind when he knocks at the door and says, "Are you OK? Can we talk?"

I come out with my Givenchy evening dress. It's a classic short, black dress. It hugs my frame nicely and makes me look elegant. When he sees me, he says, "Wow, you look amazing! Thank you for being here with me."

He stops, then I say, "Thanks. And I appreciate the invite."

He continues, "About my profession of love for you, I didn't mean to scare you. I was a bit overcome with emotions. But you are very special to me, and I don't want to scare you off."

I breath in and say, "OK, it's just I'm not used to people saying they love me that's all." He looks at me and smile. Then Pierre knocks at the door, so we leave it at that. I try to put it out of my head as he did not expect a response from me.

Our dinner goes smoothly as neither of us bring up what he said earlier. We pass the next few days doing the tourist thing around the city. Karen and his mom join us at some of our excursions like the Museum of Glass and the Art Museum. I love the art scene in this city. During the week we spend some time with just his family. On

Thursday we go out for dinner with his mom, sister and dad at a swanky restaurant and on Friday we have lunch at his parent's house. The week flies by quickly and regardless of my hesitance and that dreaded word, I embrace his family.

Chapter 20

On Saturday, we get to his parents' house, which is elegantly decorated out with mini lights leading up the driveway. I remember Karen saying their theme is 'A Night Under the Stars'. As we walk around to the backyard these twinkling lights are everywhere and really highlights the theme. It's tastefully done.

We are greeted right away by Karen giving each of us a huge bear hug. I tell her, "The place looks wonderful! How can I help?"

James eyes me and says, "Oh no my lady, I intend for you to dance with me!"

Karen giggles and says, "We are all done. Everything is in place. Go mingle!"

I wasn't trying to escape him, I just wanted to be helpful. OK, maybe I was trying to get away. Everything is tastefully done, and many people are in attendance. I see the aunt and uncle, so we go over to say hello.

Mr. and Mrs. Donaldson see us and come over. I go up to Mr. Donaldson and give him a big hug saying, "Happy birthday!"

He says, "Thank you for being here with my son!" He gives James a wink and a pat on the back.

James says, "Dad, you look fantastic!" And they hug. It's quite endearing, unfortunately this is foreign to me as I do not have this sort of family dynamics. Emotions like hug and 'I love you' are heavily frowned upon in my upbringing.

We continue to mingle and James stays by my side all the time. I think he wants to hold my hand the whole time too, but I occasionally let go of him. I don't really need a keeper.

I meet more of his extended family, and thankfully they do not bring up who I am or simply they don't recognize my name. In any circumstance, the evening is moving smoothly.

Around eight p.m. we are seated at this huge, long table that attempts to hold us all. It's a bit of a comic site but it works! We are beside James' parents and sister.

Everyone wants a piece of James. They want to know about his career and the big city. A few people mention that he really lucked out with a girl as pretty as me. I hate compliments so I pretended not to hear and let James respond to them, as most of these comments are made to him in any case.

The vibe is nice and atmosphere is pleasant then Cindy comes over and says hi to both of us. She is wearing a very revealing dress, and compliments James by saying, "You look hot tonight. Or what does the young people say, delish!" Which makes him embarrassed and he doesn't reply, but politely smiles.

I want to ask her where is my compliment? As we are talking within this group of three, she completely ignores me. James says, "Estella loves fashion as you can tell. She helped me pick out my outfit tonight." That is true, I did choose his ensemble.

She ignores his comments and asks him, "We should go out tomorrow!" I have a feeling she is not including me in this excursion.

But James says, "I'll see our schedule and how we are doing with time." She continues to chat with James and not me for two minutes. Then James says, "Excuse me, Cindy." He turns to me and says, "I want to show you something. Come!" And we leave Cindy sitting by herself looking quite awkward.

"Where are you taking me?" I ask as we enter the house.

He responds, "Yesterday I forgot to show you my sketch pads. Would you like to see it?" I would! So, I nod enthusiastically.

He takes me again to his bedroom, which is as neat as ever. He rumbles through his closet and finds a stack of pads. Some are simple pencil sketches and others are water paints. It is impressive and he has talent. I say, "Wow these are all beautiful and should be shown to the world!"

He says, "I spent many hours creating these. They are personal to me which I don't share with anyone."

I then look around his room and say, "She wants you".

He looks at me and say, "I know; you are right. But I don't want her."

I tell him, "She is persistent!"

He says, "I don't care, and I want someone else." The chemistry is undeniable between us. He comes over and starts passionately kissing me.

I quickly hike up my dress and unzip his pants as he pushes me up against his dresser. He then inserts his hard manhood inside me. I'm so wet and he's so big and hard that it feels amazing. He goes faster and faster and I come with a loud but stifled moan and he comes right after me.

We then sink down onto his bed panicking for breadth. "That was amazing!" he tells me.

I say, "It was!" We entangle our fingers together and I turn over and kiss his cheek. Then I say, "We should go back to the party."

He says, "Yes, we should." He then kisses me on my lips. We fix our clothing before making our way down to the party.

Dinner has been served. Our food is sitting there untouched. James leads me to my seat, and we start eating. The crowd is done eating and starting to mingle. I cannot eat, but clearly James is famished. So, I tell him I'm going to find Karen and see if I can be useful. He doesn't want me to go but his family members are coming over to chat with him.

I manage to escape, so I head into the kitchen to look for Karen. She is busy talking to a chef and servers. She seems to have everything under control, so I make my way to the back garden bed just to see the stars.

As I am staring up into the sky, someone approaches me from behind. "Hi, Estella. Finally, you are away from James!" I turn around to face her. Is she kidding me? What does she possibly have to say to me?

I say, "Yes, finally. What do you want?" I don't do cat fights with girls. It's not my thing. And I don't beat around the bush either. She clearly doesn't want to be my friend and she wants James, so now what does she want from me?

"You are very direct, aren't you? Well, I guess that should be expected because you run multimillion dollar corporations." I stand there silently looking at her and waiting for her to continue, as I'm not in the mood to converse. She says, "Anyways, James is a really good guy, and I feel you are changing him. He has, what you city people would call, small town values. He's not meant to be with you. Do you even see yourself with him? Married? With children?"

She stops and expects a response from me. I'm getting tired from listening to her, so I say, "Why are you still talking to me? Take this up with James."

As I am turning to leave she grabs my arm, then says, "I'm not done!" I look at her hand on my arm, then she quickly removes it. "Listen, you must care a little about him, don't you? He's head over heels in love with you and I know you don't feel the same for him. Don't wait to break his heart. Just do it now."

She pauses and then says, "He's just a simple guy you can easily replace in New York. So, give him up so his family and I can pick up the pieces!" I have had enough; I need to get out of here.

I tell her with a lot of venom in my voice, "Don't ever touch me again." Then I walk away and pull out my phone and message Pierre to come get me.

I leave without saying goodbye to James or his family. My head is pounding in the car. We pull up to the hotel and I head into the room. I start packing my bags and call Pierre up to take them to car.

I cannot think; my head is pounding! I know that woman wants James and will say anything to break us up. But what she said was all true! She hit the nail on its head. What was I thinking stringing him along like this? I will only end up hurting him more. I have already done so much damaged! I need to stop right at this moment.

My phone buzzes, I see it's James, but I'm going to ignore it. I cannot speak or see him right now. I need to leave.

In the car I call the concierge desk and say, "Please keep the room as long as Mr. Donaldson needs it. As well, I need you to get a first-class plane ticket for James Donaldson's to New York. It needs to be open as well. Charge everything to the credit card on file. Thank you."

I am going home without James. We were schedule to go home Monday night, but I think it's best to just cut ties with him right away. I have really fucked up this and more importantly hurt James. I didn't want to hurt him. I never did really. Now he's in love with me, and I'm a cold-hearted bitch that can never give him what he's looking for. He deserves so much better than me. At the room I left him a little note that reads:

I'm so sorry, but I never meant to hurt you or to allow this to get so serious. I'm not capable of being loved or loving back. I'm sorry I came into your life. You will get over me. There are a lot of better women out there!

Take care:

E. H.

I think that will be enough for now. He will get over me; in time he will.

Chapter 21

It's fall in New York, and I am throwing myself into work. It's been one month since that night in Tacoma, Washington and the last time I saw James. I try not to think of him, and God knows I have been keeping myself busy. He constantly leaves voice messages and texts and even emails.

The first week was so painful. He came to my house a few times and Pierre told him I do not want to see him. He sent 102 messages and fifty voice mails. I ignored all of them and after that I started deleting them. If I read them, it would have broken my heart so anything that comes from his account I forward to my trash.

And here I am being quite busy with my two companies and trying not to think about him. I'm going to be selling the telecommunication company to Mr. Yamamoto. His business mantra is amazing and if anyone will take over my baby it needs to be him. We are currently working out the purchase. The price is ridiculously out of the ballpark and considering who he is and the price, I could not say no.

My team and I are revamping Havisham international. I will be transferring most of my employees over to that company including my VP and Cassandra. I also hired a personal assistant, Giovanna. She has been very helpful keeping me organized personally.

I would be lying to myself if I say I'm happy. After that fatal night at James's dad birthday, I have cried myself to sleep every night since. I miss him, and really want to see him again and feel him and talk to him. But eventually I will stop feeling all this. And then what? I'm sure he has moved on and found a 'normal' girl to spend his time with that wants what he wants. I know he wants marriage and babies. I'm not capable of that. I don't have any sort of maternal instincts.

No, what I did is for the best. I save him from further heartbreak and save myself from dealing with love or family; concepts which I'm unfamiliar with anyways. Thanks to his ex, she reminded me who I really am.

I will get over this because I'm strong. I don't need love or a man or a partner or a family. I want to live my life like Adela—free from family and heartbreak. I might consider getting a ward. Maybe adopt a child or something. No, that's a silly idea, unlike Adela I don't want a spawn.

I wonder when the texts and voice mails will stop or have they already stopped? I cannot keep thinking about him. He needs to be in the past with Tom and the rest of them. They don't mean anything to me. But James is different, does that mean I love him? Is that the right descriptor? Am I capable of that? No, no—it was just lust plus I felt we got along well because we were friends. He understood me like no other, not even Adela, and I think I understood him as well. So why did I leave? Because I knew I couldn't continue this. It would eventually end. If not by me, he would leave me because I am not capable of giving him what he wants and that would destroy me. So, it's better to cut it off now rather than to prolong it.

Yes, that's why I did it. I need to toughen up and get him out of my head! I made the right decision. Besides Adela has been staying with me for the past week. She is really frail and sick, and she wants to be around me.

Arthur and his daughter were tormenting her at the estate in New Hampshire. She has sent him a cease-and-desist letter, and they have been quiet ever since. Her trip to New York with Berta is for her to spend some time with me; I insisted on it. I don't mind because my home is spacious enough and she can have her privacy, and in any case I feel lonely.

If James was in my life, she would not approve and she would think I was being silly to keep him for so long. She, of course, would be right. It's a bit awkward going home to her again, but I'm OK with it as there isn't anyone that I'm keeping from her in my life.

Work brings me temporary joy. Cassandra and even Giovanna see it. I'm miserable and I've become even colder. I keep to myself, and I do not find pleasure in anything besides work.

If one thinks that I was devoid of emotions before, now it's a whole new level. I speak to my employees with basic respect, no emotions. I let my assistant and VP deal with employee relations. As for my clients, Mr. Darcy handles some, but I'm still the face of both companies, so I attend all the meetings and now I'm extra diligent with everything, which means I'm all business and cold. I can't help it. My universe is dark, so this is how I deal with everything that touches me.

It's November and Cassandra is in my office taking notes for the sale of my telecommunication company. I dictate to her the agenda for the contract which will take another week for me to put together the paperwork.

After she is done taking notes, she looks at me and says, "I'm sorry, Estella."

I look up to her and ask, "Why are you apologizing? Why are you sorry?"

She continues loudly with, "You are so broken! And miserable. Why don't you call him! Or at least go on a date with someone else. You will wither up and die if you don't!" This is extreme and uncharacteristic, as she is shaking.

I tell her in a quiet and restrained cold voice, "Cassandra, I appreciate the work you do here, and you get compensated for it. However, stay out of my personal life. Thank you, that's all." And with that she gets up and leaves.

At home, Adela is reading one of my Dickens novels in the study. She likes Victorian novels. I go into the study and tell her, "I'm sad!"

She cocks her head to the side and say, "What's wrong? What is there to be sad about?" I go across the room and sit down beside her. We do not usually show any sort of affections or emotions, and this takes her by surprise.

I hold her feeble, cold, old hands and say, "I'm lonely and I miss him." We have never discussed James, but I know she knows everything about him.

After a while she says, "It's for the best you cut ties with him. He was no good for you. Find another arrogant jackass to taunt and that will make you feel better." She then smiles at me and pulls her hands away.

I go into the kitchen, and she feebly follows me. She comments, "What's wrong, Estella?"

I tell her, "Nothing. I'm just tired." Then I grab a yogurt from the fridge and go to my room.

It's early, so I pull my calendar and work schedule out and start organizing my week. Then I respond to a few emails. Suddenly tears start springing from my eyes and run down my cheeks.

I roll over onto my pillow and start sobbing into to it. I miss him so much and I know I love him. As much as I want to disbelieve and deny it, I know I love him.

***

Two days later, Ms. Havisham and I are having tea in the dining room, when Pierre rings up to say Tom Calloway is here to see me. I say into the phone, "Tom! Do not let him up!"

And before I can say another word to Pierre, Adela tells me calmingly, "I've invited him. Send him up please." I look at her, but there is just a blank stare at me.

I tell Pierre, who's still on the phone, "Adela has invited him, so send him up." Then I hang up and look at Adela.

I say, "why did you invite that man here?"

She calmly looks at me and says, "You have been too sad as of late. It's not becoming. Don't be cross!"

I stop myself from yelling at her as the front door opens and in walks Tom. He looks good and a bit humble, not as arrogant as per the usual with him. Adela follows me to the foyer to greet him.

"Hi Estella, Ms. Havisham," he says nonchalantly.

I say, "Tom, why are you here?"

Then he responds, "To visit both of you. Adela said I can." We both look at this meek, old lady.

She finally says, "Welcome, Tom. I'm happy you took me up on my invitation. How are you doing?"

Why is she doing this? She has an agenda that obviously has to do with me, but what? She doesn't particularly like Tom, and she was quite pleased when I divorced him. She spoke about deflating his ego and making him grovel. She got a lot of pleasure out of his suffering. But now why is she inviting him over?

"Estella, you look like a goddess! And Adela you look lovely." Tom says and distracts me from my reverie. OK. What's going on? I'm going to try and play along. Tom doesn't particularly like Adela either, so they are obviously planning something.

After a short pause she says, "Thanks, Tom. Well, I think it's fitting that you two should go out to dinner tonight! I would come, but I don't want to catch my death in the cold!" I look at her and instantly knows she wants to set us up again. But why? He's a douche.

"No, I can't. I'm quite busy tonight. I have work to do." I say casually.

Tom says, "We can go for a quick dinner, and I'll bring you back early! So how about it?"

I then say, "Tom the last time I saw you I told you that I was not interested and to leave me alone. So why are you back?"

That's me for being blunt! Adela this time responds with, "Estella, stop this mopping around. You have been so melancholic for the last month that I cannot take it any more. You won't go out with any one of those young men I sent to your office. At least now let Tom take you out to dinner! He's familiar and a known person! You need to get out of this runt that you are in!" Yes, Adela has tried to match me up with several assholes, which I declined.

She stops and they both look at me. Tom breaks the silence by saying, "Estella, I love you so much and I see that you are sad. I want to help!"

I say without thinking, "You can't!"

And Tom's responds with, "He couldn't have meant much to you. I'm willing to leave my wife for you and possibly destroy my political career for you." I can see Adela taking pleasure from this profession of love by Tom.

I simply say, "No thank you, Tom. I don't want your love or anyone else's. So, stop this!"

He continues, "You think you love him! He was a jackass! A fucking low life!" I see the infamous Callaway's anger boiling over.

And I say, "Don't you dare say anything about him. You never knew him and he's ten times the man you are. Now get out of my house!" At that moment I press my call button to Pierre, but he's already standing at the door, I guess he must have heard us.

Adela says, "Estella, stop this. He's a no body. You did the right thing putting him out of your life. Now you need to move on, and Tom loves you!"

I don't look at her, but I say, "Neither of you will tell me what to do. I'm an adult and will choose for myself. Tom, we are done. Go home to your wife. I do not want to be with you ever. And Adela, I choose for myself, so stay out of my affairs!" With that I glance at Pierre to get Tom out and I storm up to my room.

I hear Adela calling for me and Pierre telling Tom to leave, then I shut my door. I feel sick, as if I'm going to throw up; I quickly head to the bathroom and vomit into the sink. My head is spinning. I go to my bed and slump down and bury myself in the duvet.

Chapter 22

Two months later, and Mr. Yamamoto and several Japanese chairmen are proprietors of the telecommunication company. My baby is gone, but she is in good hands.

I'm not sad about this decision as it was for the best. I will dedicate all my time and energy now to Havisham international. I have procured office sites in London and Tokyo and more in the near future. It's a great company and will become greater.

I am still struggling with my personal life. I have lost twenty-lbs since the breakup. I'm living on soups and crackers. I still miss him; I really thought time will mend this, but it hasn't!

Adela went home a week ago. Her health is getting worse, and she wants to be around her familiar home and long-time friends, so I did not object. I will go visit soon.

I feel alone and helpless. I have many potential suitors, but they mean nothing to me. I do not want to go out or meet anyone; I don't want sex or even to converse personally with anyone. I live through my work, and that's all the interaction I have. I go to balls and many beautiful galas all over the world to promote Havisham Int. but they are hallow and just business; they do not affect me personally. I eat alone in my big house, then go to sleep.

Severally times Cassandra and Giovanna have encouraged me to go out with them or even after work for a glass of wine, but I just can't bring myself to be social. I have not gone to church either. I don't deserve to be in God's house, so I stay away.

I hate myself for how I ruined Tom and the other men I strung along, including James and of course the first one, Philip. I know I purposefully hurt each and every single one of them and for that I hate myself. But I was never dishonest with any of them.

James was different than all of them because I truly think I love him. If this is what love feels like, then I am in love with him.

I need to talk to him. I cannot keep living like this. I buzz Cassandra and tell her I'm leaving the office for a quick walk. I'll be back soon.

I walk down to James' office, the old one, as he did not move to the new building. I'm guessing that's because I own it. I step into to the deli across the street and sit at a table that has a good view of the front doors. I don't know what I am doing or why I'm stalking this man, but apparently, I am.

I order a coffee and croissant. I peck at the croissant and sip the hot liquid while watching the doors. An hour later, the waitress startles me by asking if I would like anything else. I tell her no and I want the bill. I leave and go back to my office.

I do this for two weeks straight. I just sit at the same table watching the front doors. I have never seen him enter or leave, and I know I wouldn't because I always come at the same time.

Today, I decide to go up to his office. I see his secretary who I vaguely remember from Mr. Templeton's deal. However, she clearly remembers me because as soon as she sees me, she says, "Ms. Havisham! How are?"

I tell her, "I'm well, is Mr. Donaldson available?"

She says, "He's completely booked this afternoon, but as soon as Cindy leaves you can go in between his next meeting." She smiles as though she is doing me a favour.

I look at her blankly and say, "Thanks, but it's OK, I'll come another time." And before she can even respond, I turn and leave as quickly as I can. *What the fuck was I thinking? Cindy! Fuck! Of course, I deserve this... karma. Fuck!*

It's been six months since I saw him. Why would he wait around that long for me? But I did for him. I thought about him every single day and fall asleep in tears thinking of his touch and longing for this man.

I get back to my office and close the door behind me. I buzz Cassandra and have her cancel all my meetings for that day. I message Pierre and tell him to get the jet ready because I'm going to Ms. Havisham.

I can't think of anywhere or anyone else to turn to. I feel sick, but there is a knock at my door. I open it and its Cassandra.

I see him in front of her desk. He's in a navy suit and he looks impeccable. He comes closer, and our eyes lock onto each other.

"Cassandra, that will be all," I say feebly to her. He enters my office and I lock the door. I look at him and him to me. We say nothing.

I break the silence by saying, "Why are you here?"

He looks at me and says, "Why did you come to my office?"

Because I want you back, but I say, "To say hello because I was in the neighbourhood."

Something is off about him, he's struggling as he says, "You should not have left."

I interrupt him from continuing and say, "You were busy. It was not urgent; besides you were with Cindy." Yes, I'm direct and to the point.

He then says, "Why did you leave on Aug. twenty-three at my dad's birthday without saying goodbye?"

I am unprepared for this but say, "Well, Cindy made some good points to me back then. I wasn't the woman for you and it was an easier and cowardly way to break up with you without having a confrontation." That's the truth.

He asks coldly, "What did Cindy say to you?" Why does it matter?

I say, "Only the truth… I was ruining your life and I was not right for you. So why bother stringing you along, just leave now. So, I did."

He takes a deep breath, "OK, I'm engaged to her." This hits me hard. The room is spinning… the next thing I know I open my eyes and I'm in a room with Cassandra and Pierre.

I cannot move or breathe properly. There are tubes hooked up to me. I try to motion to Cassandra to take them off, but she ignores me. I am too weak to say anything to her. I hear James' voice in the background saying, "I need to get in."

And someone saying, "Sir, there are too many people here as it is. Who are you?"

I hear James saying, "I'm a friend. It's important that I be there for her. I need to be in there with her." Then I must have fallen asleep again.

I wake up and my head just hurts. No one is in the room, but there are lots of flowers. I feel drained. A nurse then comes in and she starts to check my vitals. She says, "Good morning, Estella. You look much better. How are you?"

I open my mouth and very feebly say, "How long have I been here?" The nurse looks at me and smiles. She is young and pretty.

She says, "Three days, are you thirsty?" *Three days!*

I say to her, "Why am I here, what's wrong with me?"

She then sets my pillow properly and says, "Don't agitate yourself. You were exhausted and dehydrated. You fainted three days ago."

What! I don't remember much, I continue, "How is this possible?"

The nurse goes on, "You need to eat as well." She is gentle when she speaks and calm. I like that.

I ask, "Where is my phone?"

She responds with, "You can have that later. Right now, you need to regain your strength!"

I then tell her, "I'm thirsty."

She brings a glass with a straw to me, and I slowly suck the water out. She says, "You are doing really well."

I take the opportunity to ask, "When can I leave?"

And she smiles but says, "Soon." Then she leaves.

I look around me and notice everything that's in the room. I have three huge stuff bears, twelve bouquets of beautiful floral arrangements and a stack of cards on a table. But no one is here with me. I feel alone and a little depress.

After thirty mins, a young man walks in with my nurse. He's curt with her and goes through my chart with his fingers. He then says in a very condescending tone, "How are we feeling, Ms. Havisham?" I don't like him.

I say, "Like a ton of bricks fell on me. When can I go home?" He looks at me and smiles.

Then after reviewing my chart again he says, "Well, your vitals look good. You were very dehydrated and there was hardly any food in your system. The IV has improved all that. I'll say maybe tomorrow, if you keep improving."

With that, he turns his back to me and is about to leave when I say, "I want out of here by this afternoon, sir."

He looks at me and says, "When Dr. Neil returns, we shall see."

Then it dawns on me that this man is not my doctor but my new nurse! Honestly, I think I'm losing it. I say to him, "Are you my new nurse? Where is the young girl?"

He replies, "Yes, I am and her shift ended. Did you think I was your doctor?"

And I say, "Yes, please have Dr. Neil come and see me right away when he gets in. Thanks." And then I close my eyes!

After the hospital lunch that I peck at but had to eat most of it because, Henry, my new nurse was watching me, Dr. Neil makes his appearance. He's a middle-aged man with the name tag Dr. Neil on it. He is courteous and nice enough, but I get to the point right away.

"So, when can I leave?"

He looks at me and says, "Ms. Havisham, I'm so happy you are in my care, and I want to ensure that you are fully recovered before discharging you." From his diplomacy and tone, he knows exactly who I am. I donate to the sick kids wing of this hospital, plus my name is on a wing of the building!

"I feel much better since I woke up. I can recover in the comfort of my own home." I retort.

He smiles and says, "You don't need to stress or work yourself up right now. You need a vacation to just relax and clear your mind, eat well and drink lots of healthy fluids."

Great so discharge me then! Instead, I say, "That can all be arranged. So kindly discharge me, please." I smile and he smiles back.

He knows I don't take no for an answer, so he replies, "OK, the earliest I can do is in the afternoon. But I will prescribe some medicine and routine that you need to follow for the next couple of weeks, OK."

I respond with, "Sure thing."

And he says, "I must say you are even more beautiful in person!"

I pretend to blush and say, "Thanks." Then as he checks my vitals and measures the IV while, I quickly look around for my bag. Then I ask him to kindly get my phone for me. I call Pierre to come.

Literally five minutes later, I hear a raucous outside my private room between Pierre and Henry. Pierre opens my door and both Dr. Neil and I stare at him and Henry, who says, "Sir, you can't just come in here as you please! As you can see the doctor is in with her."

Of course, Pierre's response is, "So?"

Which I follow with, "I told him to come!" And Dr. Neil says, "Its fine, Henry. He can come in. I'm almost done." Then Henry and Dr. Neil leave, but not before telling Pierre the particulars of my rest and discharge.

I tell Pierre as soon as they leave to lock the door. He sits beside me and says in a very unusually sweet voice, "Don't you ever scare me like that again!"

I smile and say, "Please get me out of here!"

Then he says, "You need to make some changes. Promise me to eat and drink more and stop stressing over work so much!"

I appreciate his friendly tone and concern. This is probably the first time I've ever seen this side of him. I say, "I plan to!" And I mean that. I need to start taking care of myself and not being so depressed over a man. I don't need James.

Pierre gets everything ready for me to leave and has packed up all my belongings with the help of Giovanna and Cassandra, who came while Pierre and I were gathering my belongings. My check out is around five p.m. promptly where Dr. Neil will come and officially discharge me. I am anxious to go home because the last thing I want is for the press to find out.

At four-thirty, James enters my room. Initially, I thought it was Pierre, but it's James. I say, "Hi, what are you doing here?"

He responds with, "I am worried about you. How are you?" I don't feel angry or depress any more, I feel renewed, but weak.

My response is chilly, "I'm fine, no need to worry about me." My walls are back up and I don't really want this man any more in my life.

He says, "I'm sorry, Estella. Things went horribly wrong between us! But I wanted to say you are the love of my life. I don't want to lose you." What the fuck is this man saying. I really don't have the stamina to deal with this right now. But I want closure.

I say, "I don't understand what sort of game you are playing. But I have resigned. Please accept my good wishes for you and your fiancé." I say this without resentment or gall because I sincerely just want the best for him right now as he is a good person essentially. And this is probably the best move for him.

He looks at me and says, "I don't blame you for hating me or never wanting to see me again. After you left and refused all my attempts to see you, I broke down and Cindy was there to help me through it. She proposed the engagement and I agreed. My life was over without you, so who cares who I got married to or spend the rest of it with."

I cut him off as I don't want to hear this, "James stop, please. This is too much, it's done and you don't need to explain your decisions to me. You have moved on and I wish you all the best. I'm a horrible person for just leaving. I clearly have commitment phobia, so thank you for putting up with me for that long. I think Cindy is definitely many steps above me. So, enjoy your life. I couldn't give you what you need and deserve!" I end it there and I truly don't mean any malice towards him. I just want him to be happy.

He says after a minute, "Estella, you have no idea what you mean to me. I feel alive when I'm with you. Forget the money or the trips, it was always just you and me! It's an extraordinary feeling that I have never felt before with anyone. I want that. Estella, I want you! As for Cindy, I guess she is a rebound, unfortunately. I'm not proud of myself but it happened. I was depressed and lonely and just miserable and she was literally always there!" I try to say something that it's for the best, but he continues, "I don't love her. I need and want you, exactly the way you are. I know you are fucked up! Really fucked up, but I want that. I want to hear your laughs and insecurities and bossiness. I want all of it and I'm not delusional about who you are either!" My insecurities!

He continues, "I know you love me even if you don't want to admit it. I feel it when we are together. The happiest days of my life are when I spend them with you. I'm so sorry I turned to Cindy. That was a huge error in my judgement. Please forgive me for that!" I remind myself that I really don't do love or forgiveness!

I breathe in and out hard then I muster up the energy to say, "This is a lot to deal with right now. I'm clearly not feeling well. Please stop by tomorrow at my home to discuss this matter further when I get a chance to think it over." I've just impressed myself as to how grown up and level-headed I sound! I don't want to say something I'll regret or make a rash decision, so I'm treating this as a business deal.

He agrees, apologizes again and leaves. Then Cassandra and Pierre come into my room. She says, "We didn't want to interrupt." With a smile on her face. I don't say anything as I'm tired and just want to go home.

Chapter 23

I sleep all the way home and then I have a hot shower and some actual dinner that Felix made, while Cassandra watches me finish. Even Pierre pops in to ensure I eat everything. After Cassandra leaves, Mrs. Anderson helps me up to bed and I sleep the whole night through.

The next morning, I wake up as a new person. I feel alive and rejuvenated. I check the time and it's ten a.m. I slept in and that's OK because everything can wait.

I get showered and dressed then go down to the kitchen where Felix has prepared me a delicious omelette with toast, pancakes, and fresh orange juice! I eat as much as I can then I go into my study.

I love going over my classical collection of Victorian novels. I think what would Ms. Bennet do in my situation or Emma? Then I go through my Shakespeare and Chaucer works. I read over a selection from the Canterbury Tales called The Wife of Bath because it's so beautifully written.

After an hour or so I head into my office and check my emails. There is a lot! But I have arranged with Casandra and my VP to handle most of them. I remember Ms. Havisham so I check my voice mail and of course there are two from her.

She knows about my hospitalization, and she is worried. Before falling ill, I was planning on going there for a visit, maybe I still will. I dial her number. "Hi Adela, its Estella."

She says, "My child are you OK? What happened?" I then proceed to tell her about my mishaps and doctor's recommendations. The call is amicable and lasts for twenty mins.

I then head to the living room where Mrs. Anderson has informed me that lunch will be ready in ten mins and Mr. Donaldson is waiting for me in the foyer. I recollected myself and went into the powder room to splash my face with water.

I think I'm ready for this conversation with him. But what do I want? I'm still not sure. I know who I am and what I'm capable of, but these pesky feelings keep shrouding my judgement which I do not like. Regardless, I need to put some closure to this and to him.

I walk into the foyer and I see him sitting there. I say, "Hi. Thank you for coming."

He gets up and says, "Thank you for seeing me." He looks tired and drained.

I tell him, "I think we need to address this in order to move forward. So come into my office and we can talk privately." I lead the way into my office, and we sit. I ask, "Would you like something to drink or eat?" The business-like way in which I'm dealing with him is not natural and feels forced, but I don't want any cloud of judgement.

He says, "No, thank you." Then sits opposite me.

I start, "OK, James, I think it's important for you to understand that I really did or do care about you. However, is that love? I wouldn't know because I've never been in love. As well, I can't give you the life and relationship you deserve and want." He tries to interrupt me, but I wave him to stop.

I continue, "I have been very unfair to you. To leave you without warning is quite unfair. And you moved on. This is reasonable and acceptable. I don't harness any resentment to you because you moved on."

I pause for a second and James quietly adds, "Why did you come back?"

I want to be honest with him and myself, "Because I was foolishly hoping that you were still single and might be interested in giving us another shot. That was unfair of me because my makeup/idea of love hasn't changed. So, I think I would have done you more harm because I don't think I can give you love or marriage or a family."

I pause so this sinks into him. I then say, "It hurts to hear you have moved on with, Cindy, of all people. But after thinking it over, I know it's for the best." I stop because I know what I have said is honest.

He then says, "OK, is it my turn?"

I nod and say, "Yes."

He continues, "I've listened to all what you just said, and I had a lot of time to consider everything. So, this is not a rash decision. I don't love Cindy, so I broke off our engagement two days ago."

I gasp saying, "Oh no!"

He continues, "It's really for the best. I have done her a lot of harm by agreeing to marry her when I fully knew I did not love her or wanted to spend my life with her. Marrying her would have been wrong. She also knew that I did not love her too."

He pauses then continues, "Estella, I know you think that you are not capable of love. But I completely disagree. What you have shown me, and I have felt from you over the course of knowing you was for a lack of a better term, magical! Estella, you can fight it as much as you want but you need to admit what we had and still do have is a strong bond. Whether that is love, you can decide. But Estella, what I do know for a fact is that I do not want anyone else but you. And if you keep resisting me then we will both end up old and lonely, until we die because I will not date or be with anyone else. Or we can see where this goes. I want to be with you, although we might end up killing each other, but at least we can say we tried. As for marriage and kids—I don't want any of that with another person, so if you cannot give me that, then it is OK. You are quiet, and I think I'm done."

At that, he braces back onto the wing tip chair and breadths in heavily. He's right; I can deduce that we do have a strong bond. I cannot force him to be with someone else, or marry any other, so what's the harm in continuing to see him or hang out with him? He knows my ability to love or not love in this case. As well, he is right I have missed him more than anything else! Maybe that is love.

I start after a long pause, "OK, I'm willing to give us another go. But no promises and no pressure. If I grow tired of you, I will leave and of course the same goes for you." He comes over and hugs me! To feel him again is exquisite! I run my hand over his chest and that electricity just sparkles all over me.

Before letting go of him I say, "I've missed you, but I'm very upset at you!"

He looks me in the eyes and says, "Cindy?"

I tell him, "Of all the girls, you had to go back to her!"

He moans slightly, "She means nothing to me. I've cut all ties with her. I only turned to her because she came to New York and practically saw me every day and was always there, when I was lonely and depress."

I pull away, "Don't blame her. You allowed it to happen."

And he says, "You were gone for five months! You wouldn't answer my calls or see me or respond to the hundreds of messages I sent you. I thought you would never come back." I know I need to get over this. He continues, "You need to forgive me. I only want you and no one else. I swear this on my life!"

I hug him and I do believe and trust him. I tell him, "OK, I forgive you and just so you know this is the first for me. I never forgive!" With that he kisses me deeply. Oh, how I have missed his lips and tongue.

He picks me up and lays me down on the desk. Then he rips my blouse open. He then proceeds to caress my breasts and kiss each of them. Then he says with a grin,

"How I've missed them!" Then he comes to undo my skirt and pulls it off. My panties are pink with little flowers on them. He rips them off with his teeth then spreads my legs wide.

He starts licking my clit and I just melt! I come hard and fast. Then he enters me and starts to go faster and faster. He comes and I orgasm again.

We pick ourselves up and go to my bedroom where we crawl into bed. I tell him, "I love it when you are inside me."

He entangles my fingers with his and tells me, "I love being inside you." He gently kisses me then says, "I never want to lose you again!"

I look at him and say, "I don't want to lose you." Then it hits me—Adela! "There is a problem. It's Adela, she is really sickly now and will never approve of us."

He contemplates then says, "What are you going to do?"

I ask, "What do you think I should do?"

He thinks again then says, "I know she is your only family, but you cannot allow her to separate us!"

I giggle and say, "I know! I wasn't planning to. But I need her to meet you and for her to see what I see in you!" Yes, that might work. Maybe she will see that James is truly good for me and then let it go that he's not arrogant or has a certain status in our society. And maybe she will understand my feelings for him and accept that I care about him! It's worth a try since, I have no other solutions!

Chapter 24

James and I spend the next few weeks enwrap in each other. My health improves and my overall disposition becomes happier.

Cassandra and Giovanna comment on my change and happier outlook on life on several separate occasions. My business soars. Havisham international is doing well in Europe and Asia. We are expanding and I am delegating more.

One afternoon, I decide to come home early to make the bedroom and family room romantic so to speak. I was arranging flowers and setting the lights, when Pierre messages me saying Adela is on her way up!

Fuck Adela! I get to the door in time to see Adela being wheeled in by Berta and two other caregivers. "Why are you in a wheelchair?"

She responds with, "Why are you at home from work?"

I ignore this question and ask, "Are you OK?"

She gives me the 'I know what you have been up to look,' then she says, "I fell. But I'm here now, Estella, and I've been hearing many things." Berta gives me a sympathetic look and I smile at her. There is no time for niceties between us on this occasion.

Although I have called her twice in the past two weeks, I neglected to mention James, but I knew she knew he was back in my life.

"Come, Adela. We can get to that later. Are you hungry?" I grab my phone and is about to message James about maybe staying out a little, but of course in he walks!

"Hi, James! Adela has come for a visit!" my voice is high pitched and shaky as the air fills with tension.

Adela chimes in with, "Mr. Donaldson, wonderful just the person I was hoping to come through those doors. Come on in."

James has flowers in his hands, clearly, he wants a romantic evening as well! James greets her with, "Mrs. Havisham, it's nice to finally meet you!" He extends his hand but Adela ignores him.

I interject with, "Adela be nice. This is James' home as well." She gives me a look, so I go and stand beside James. I plan to protect him from her tyranny.

Berta assists her out of the wheelchair then takes her leave with the others. As I have come to understand James, I know what a nice person he is, unlike what Adela stands for. She is all about hatred and money. She is as snobby as they come. I, of course, was taught to view the world like this. This was why my marriage to Tom was welcomed.

I need to protect James from her. He says, "Ms. Havisham, please come sit. I'm sure your journey was long. I'm James Donaldson. I have heard a lot about you."

Adela stares at him then responds with a contrive smile, "Yes, I have travelled a long way to be here. So, I will sit down, Mr. Donaldson." She then walks over to the living room couch and makes a big flourish before she sits down.

I interject by asking, "Is there something I can get you? Tea? Or something to eat? Water?"

The contrive smile reappears! I'm in so much trouble! Then she says, "No, I don't want anything." Then she looks at James and says, "I know who you are." Then she stops. I go sit beside her and hold her feeble hand. She squeezes mine then says, "What are you doing?"

My head begins to hurt, but I say, "What do you mean?" She is just addressing me now, and I want James to be in this conversation. He knows much of my dealings with Adela and he supports me but I know he has too much decorum to be rude to her. I say, "Adela, why are you here? What are you doing?"

She looks at me then at James and says, "You know why I'm here. What are you doing with him?" Here we go!

I stand up and back away from her, then I tell her, "Adela, James is my partner. We are living together, and we care about each other. I want to be with him! So that's what I'm doing with him." There is anger in my voice and she knows it.

James says, "Let's stay calm. Ms. Havisham I deeply care about Estella and promise you that I would never hurt her."

She looks at James with disgust which pains me to see, then she says, "You are not good enough for her. She is a Havisham!"

I stop her from continuing by saying, "Stop this, Adela. No one cares about a name or family heritage now. James is a good person and he's the best thing to happen to me. Can't you see that? Stop being so snobby." She does not say anything so I continue, "James is a good person from a decent family. He's educated and earns his own money. I'm not with a bum from off the street, but you know all this. You should be happy for me." I stop because my voice is shaky and I feel the tears coming.

Adela retorts with, "Estella, you are from a great family. And great family marries their own kind... other great families, not a nobody. You are not happy with him. Not truly. You are confused, come home and we will sort all this out." I'm now standing at the window admiring the sun set and small twinkling lights that are starting to be visible.

I turn to James, who is bracing against a wall. I see his face is full of sadness and I meet his eyes. I smile at him just to reaffirm everything will be all right. Then I face Adela, she looks at me with her cold eyes and I say, "I love you very much, Adela. You are the closest thing to a mother I've ever had, so I don't want to lose you. But you need to accept that I want James in my life." She knows I'm seriously, and it's less than a treat but more of a promise.

She looks around the room and then she says, "What has gotten into you? Why is he important? He just wants your money. He doesn't love you."

Before James says anything, I quickly say, "No Adela, he's different. And you will see that when you get to know him. He doesn't care about my money."

James then says, "Please believe me that I do not care about Estella's money. I would actually prefer if she had no money."

I know this about him. I know he doesn't care about my financial status and that's partly why I trust him. Adela says, "But here you are enjoying the comforts of her money. Let's see private jets, a trip to Paris, staff...""

I say, "Adela that's enough, that's my life and he accepts it. He doesn't need those things to be with me." I pause then say, "We are also not going to hurt him like we did Philip."

She looks at me and say, "Philip was a good boy. There is only a handful of things I regret, and how I treated him is one of those." I know she regrets her treatment of that young man; I believed she became fond of him all those years back, but she still went ahead and made me destroy him.

With a little pause, I continue with, "And he's not like Tim Compeyson." That's my ace!

***

Timothy Compeyson was the young man that Adela Havisham was in love with when she was eighteen. Her father was against their union as he was the boy from the wrong side of the track. He wanted to be a contractor like his father, and by the Havisham standards they were poor.

The Compeysons were contractors hired by Mr. Havisham to complete the deck adjacent to the right-wing garden. Mr. Compeyson would bring his teenage son to help his staff with the job. As soon as Adela saw him, she was hooked. Apparently, Tim was a very handsome young man.

They quickly became secret friends and then lovers. Mr. Havisham at first was not aware. So, for several months this torrid affair occurred right under his nose.

One afternoon, Adela went into her father's office and told him that she was in love with this boy and was engaged to be married to him. Mr. Havisham dragged his daughter to the ground and told her if she dared to see that boy again, he would kill her.

Adela was very close to her parents, especially her father, she was his favourite. This was hard for her to do, but she wanted to be with Tim, even if it meant running away and giving up all of her inheritance for love.

One night, she packed a small bag and snuck out of the house. She went all the way to the rougher part of town where Tim lived. She had been there before as this was a rendezvous area for their love.

To avoid Mr. Havisham, Tim took Adela to his aunt's house not too far away. Over the next couple of days Adela arranged her secret wedding. On the day of the event, Adela wore this beautiful white wedding dress which some believed she stole from her mother's closet. A few people were in attendance and all confessed how beautiful she looked. Apparently when Adela ran away, Mr. Havisham told the whole community including Tim's father that he had disinherited Adela and they can keep her. Of course, Adela only wanted love and Tim; money was not important to her at that time.

As she walked down the isle with this beautiful, laced dress but Tim was nowhere to be seen. At the alter it was reported that she waited for two hours sobbing and sobbing until her maid took her back to her parents' home. She cried and screamed for Tim for days in her bedroom. Then finally news broke that Tim ran away and had married another girl after hearing that Adela was disinherited.

This crushed Adela's heart and she vowed that she would never love another man in her life. She stayed inside her parents' house for one year and some said she kept that wedding dress on that whole time. Her father, of course, never disinherited her and as a matter-of-fact she became closer to him. She devoted herself to her parents and refused all marriage offers. As the years past, she became a bit of a hermit and wore only black in public. By all circumstance Tim killed Adela's heart, and love was gone from her forever.

***

Even his name hits her hard. She finally then says, "Men are all alike. They don't care about you!"

I say, "Don't project or group all males in the same category. People are different. Get to know James before you judge him." Of course, her affair with Tim proves she did not have good judgement, but I don't bring this up.

James then adds, "I know it's been a long day for all of us, especially you Ms. Havisham. I think we can continue this tomorrow after a good night's sleep?" Not a bad suggestion but I know Adela isn't done yet.

She says to us, "I'm going home tonight. Estella, learn from my error in judgement. I was going to throw it all away on an intuition I had about a charming young man. I was wrong, and so are you. I'm going back to my home. I suggest when you regain your senses come and see me."

"Adela, I have my full capacity and I love him. I want to be with him, and this will not change. You need to accept it because I want you in my life." Yes, I do love him! This is the first time I'm willing to admit this to myself and publicly. Unfortunately, with that she gets up and gathers her things. Our conversation is over. I need to give her time to accept us. I cannot push her or force her to accept him, she will just resent me. So, I let her go.

I call Berta, and with the others we take her downstairs but before her car comes I tell her, "He's different; I am getting a second chance. I do love him."

She looks at me and say, "I hope you don't get hurt like I was." Then she kisses me for the second time in my life. The first was when I was a little girl and my aunt was mean to me and made me cry. That's when I know she loves me. This time it's her way to say I hope you are right and goodbye.

Her car comes and she is gone. I go back up to James. He's waiting for me in the living room. He looks agitated. I go to him and hug him. I say, "I'm sorry she is like that, but she is an old woman who's use to her own ways."

James kisses me and say, "I know. I'm not offended by her comments. I knew my lack of breeding and financial merits hindered me in her eyes. I know she has hurt you, that's what I am more concerned about."

I cuddle into his arm, then I say, "Don't be, I'll be fine. She loves me and will accept what I choose. Plus, I'm being more independent with my decisions and I'm making my own decisions."

James then looks into my eyes and say, "So you mention that you love me, was that a mistake?" I think about this before responding; I do love him—I care about him, I want to spend the rest of my life with him and I love all the little things he does; I know this is love.

I look into his eyes and say, "James Donaldson, I do love you and I want to spend the rest of my life with you, if that's OK, of course."

I smile because this takes real courage and maturity from me to admit this. James' green eyes sparkle and he has a huge smile on his face, then he says, "It's more than OK, Estella Havisham I love you so much, will you marry me?"

Ohh, wow! I quickly say, "Yes!" Without thinking. He kisses me and I'm so overjoyed by this. I pull away and say, "Is this for real?"

He looks at me and say, "Absolutely. I want to spend my whole life with you!" Then he looks gloomy and says, "I wasn't planning this proposal. I don't have a ring."

I giggle and say, "I don't care about a ring!"

He then asks again, "Are you sure you want to marry me?"

I smile and this time I think it through and say, "Yes, absolutely!"